The Last Day of a Condemned Man

The Last Day
of a Condemned Man

Victor Hugo

Translated by Geoff Woollen

ET REMOTISSIMA PROPE

100 PAGES

100 PAGES
Published by Hesperus Press Limited
4 Rickett Street, London SW6 1RU
www.hesperuspress.com

English language translation © Geoff Woollen, 1992, 2002
Introduction © Geoff Woollen, 2002
This translation first published by Oxford University Press in 1992
First published by Hesperus Press Limited, 2002

Foreword © Libby Purves, 2002
Afterword © Amnesty International, 2002

Designed and typeset by Fraser Muggeridge
Printed in the United Arab Emirates by Oriental Press

ISBN: 1-84391-007-1

CONTENTS

Foreword by Libby Purves   vii

Introduction   xi

The Last Day of a Condemned Man

    Preface to the 1832 edition   3

    The Last Day of a Condemned Man   25

    A Comedy about a Tragedy   93

    Notes   103

Afterword by Kate Allen, Amnesty International, UK   105

Biographical note   109

FOREWORD

There are a few writers whose work, though rooted in the detail of their own time and place, speaks across generations and frontiers. Victor Hugo, child of post-Revolutionary France, is one of them. His own life spanned a century of painfully evolving theories about justice and democracy: he led the field in his own time, and he continues to lead in ours. As he wrote himself, 'Social problems do not have frontiers. Humankind's wounds, those huge sores that litter the world, do not stop at the red and blue lines drawn on maps.' It is no accident that *Les Misérables* has become one of the longest-running international musicals in the late twentieth century: he himself said that the novel belonged, 'wherever children lack a book to learn from or a warm hearth, wherever women sell themselves for bread.' *The Last Day of a Condemned Man*, an earlier, shorter but equally violently felt sketch, carries the same power, and the same universality.

Yet Hugo, we should never forget, is profoundly French, and a man of his troubled times. France shows herself in the practicality that runs alongside his passion, his sense of family, the earthy humour, and in the underlying obsession with justice – the need to rehabilitate the twisted, bloodstained slogan, 'Liberté, Egalité, Fraternité.' And modern France knows it. In 2002, the bicentenary of his birth, French political rivals vied comically for the honour of identification with this national hero. Lionel Jospin the socialist lined himself up with Jean Valjean, hero of *Les Misérables*. Jacques Chirac's supporters did the same, saying that Jospin was more like the venal policeman Javert. Jean-Pierre Chevènement did the same. Hugomania swept the nation's media, just as it did when the author died in 1885, and the Arc de Triomphe was draped in black velvet for an immense state funeral (attended by more than the population of Paris). Hugo had become in his lifetime almost a sacred figure: he himself told the story of how in old age, arriving home late and desperate to relieve himself, he failed to wake the concierge and was driven to urinate against the wall. A man passing upbraided him: 'How could you! Shame! In front of the house of

Victor Hugo!'

In that bicentenary spring he was hailed as the father of a united European currency – for which he did indeed campaign in 1850 – a prophet of liberal democracy. But it was the speaker of the French Senate, Christian Poncelet, who phrased it best: 'Hugo' he said, 'belongs to nobody, in that he embodies the entirety of humanity in its struggle against fatalism and the fight for progress.'

That struggle against fatalism and cynicism, and a belief in progress, is the essence of Hugo's work. Through all his political affiliations he always believed with a passion that things could be made better. Some call him 'The French Shakespeare' but he is far more of a Dickens: what marks his best work is a sort of furious, hectoring compassion, combined with a headlong Dickensian willingness to pull every emotional string in sight, and to hell with accusations of sentimentality. Fresh-cheeked little girls, childhood meadows, rays of sun falling through bars onto ragged prisoners, birds singing sweetly beyond dungeon walls, old women shivering for want of a few embers in their crock – Victor Hugo will make use of them to draw attention to the cause of justice.

This novella, *The Last Day of a Condemned Man*, is a miniature distillation of his beliefs and his imagination. He was only twenty-seven when he wrote it, and sickened by his country's continuing love affair with the guillotine, the engine of death born three years before he was. He saw the death penalty as not only cruel and gruesome but stupid; he rages at the lack of reason behind it:

'Either the man you punish has no family, no relatives, no ties that bind him in this world. In which case he has received no schooling, no education, no attention has been paid to his heart or his mind; therefore by what right do you kill this hapless orphan? You punish him because he has been dragged up, untrained and unsupported! ...His destiny is the culprit, and not he. You punish an innocent man.

'Or else the man has a family – in which case, do you believe that to slit his throat wounds him alone?... once again, you punish innocents!' (Preface)

The message could be delivered by any present-day liberal, about any extreme punishment. The scorn and satire of his Preface, and of the playlet that appeared in later editions (*A Comedy about a Tragedy*), hammer his point home. But when it comes to the diary of the condemned man himself, his touch is more delicate. Hugo's prisoner is a rounded character: baffled, angry, doubtful, maudlin and remorseful in turns, as any of us would be in his shoes.

Its strength lies in the detail, the closeness with which the prison and its denizens are conjured up. Within a few lines we are there, in the dim beam of the night-light, feeling the damp flagstones and the coarse-woven garments, wincing at the guard's courtesy ('a warder's respect reeks of the scaffold' [Chapter 5]). Like George Orwell in his famous essay about an execution in Burma, the prisoner expresses the unique horror of knowing that a body now living will soon be dead, by decree and not by nature or accident. 'Before hearing my death sentence I was aware that my lungs breathed, that my heart beat, and that my body lived in the community of other men; now I plainly saw that a barrier had sprung up between them and me. Nothing was the same as before.' (Chapter 2)

It is a story that gathers pace, as Hugo carefully increases the drama by the varying, unpredictable division into chapters. Sometimes it reaches the intensity of nightmare, as the author grapples with the incredible, impossible certainty of impending death. Sometimes it verges on black comedy, as when he discovers the desensitised uselessness of the priest who counsels only the condemned. A void at the heart of the story is deliberate: Hugo's pretence that the man is going to tell us what crime he did. The 'missing' chapter (47) would, it is supposed, tell us that he killed someone in a *crime passionnel*. In fact, its omission makes his case the stronger: Hugo does not think it matters, because whoever the law kills is either a friendless victim of circumstance, or else a loved member of a family. Either way, the innocent suffer (and in 1829, the family might well starve). Where's the sense? cries Hugo – in 1829 a young husband and father himself – in the voice of the condemned man. What in God's name is the point? And although we accept that our narrator is a murderer we have to listen: he holds the awful authority of the dying.

I first read this book over forty years ago, as a schoolchild in France. I had almost forgotten it until Geoff Woollen's fresh, slangy, demotic translation emerged to electrify a new age. The speeding up, the terror, the rage, the odd quiet lyrical passages, all came back with the same power. It is a tale of its own place and period – you cannot but see Bicêtre prison and the deadly loom of Notre-Dame over the execution square – yet at the same time it breathes a powerful, angry message to the age of the electric chair and the lethal injection in the US, and the Taliban's executions on the football ground of Kabul. And in France, too, in May 2002, almost twenty per cent of the electorate voted the National Front candidate, death penalty supporter Jean-Marie Le Pen into second place as President.

Le Pen is one politician who could never claim the mantle of his country's greatest polemic writer. The death penalty, says Hugo flatly across the centuries, is insupportable. But even those who support it should read this, and marvel at the concentrated, imaginative conviction that a young man born in a brutal age could conjure up, and hurl in rage at the powers that ran his land.

— Libby Purves, 2002

INTRODUCTION

The Last Day of a Condemned Man was published on 3 February 1829, and before the end of the month ran to further editions which included the satirical *A Comedy about a Tragedy*. Post-1832 reprints also included a long and eloquent preface.

Victor Hugo (1802–85), the author of this pseudo-diary of the thoughts and dreams of a man on death row, was a lifelong advocate of penal reform. Some of his ideas may now appear to us to be cranky and inhumane: he advocated, for instance, that the Philadelphia prison regime of up to five years' solitary confinement be extended to life for convicted murderers. Yet never, even in exile on Jersey when he vainly petitioned the Home Office on behalf of an Englishman, did he desist from involvement in penological debate. He had been but ten years old when, returning from a visit to his father, General Hugo, in Spain, he saw a man about to be garrotted and executed in Burgos, then the grisly human relics of a public crucifixion on a cross in Vitoria, soul-searing sights calculated to provoke his aversion to capital punishment, whatever the crime.

Public attitudes, however, needed to change, as the normal tendency to give the populace its bread and circuses ensured that beheadings were enacted with due pomp and ceremony. The impact was intended to be cautionary and deterrent ('to encourage the others', in Voltaire's famous formulation), but it was often contended that such spectacles led to unhealthy voyeurism. Vast crowds gathered to witness the condemned prisoner's short journey from the Conciergerie prison across the Seine and down the quays to the red-painted scaffold erected on the Place de Grève, in front of the Hôtel de Ville. Places at every available vantage point sold at a premium, as Hugo's prisoner notes (Chapter 48): 'Dealers in human blood were bawling: "Take your places."' For those in the provinces unable to attend, newspaper accounts of the decapitee's last moments were freely available, supplementing the broadsheets of the trial and judgement that were hawked in Paris itself: 'An unfortunate man's crime, his punishment, his tortures, and his final moments are turned into a commodity, a paper that is sold for a sou' (Preface of 1832). The number of the condemned cell was known, and the man taking notes on the customary *toilette* of the prisoner (Chapter 47) appears to be a reporter.

All this was proto-tabloid material, however, and other publications of the 1820s took a less ghoulish, more humanitarian interest. A daily such as the *Gazette des Tribunaux* was entirely devoted to matters of crime and punishment, and a liberal organ such as the *Constitutionnel* campaigned for greater generosity to be shown to prisoners of all categories, particularly in its regular accounts of Benjamin Appert's philanthropic prison visits. A traditional topic of tender pity was the convict departures from the multi-purpose institution of Bicêtre (Chapters 4–12), which as well as being a holding prison for those sentenced to hard labour, housed an insane asylum, and geriatric and venereal disease wards. Hugo, accompanied by the sculptor David d'Angers in 1827, was just one of the 'sightseers come from Paris' (Chapter 13) who witnessed scenes of men being permanently manacled in pairs, with the predictable result. As Michel Foucault's *Discipline and Punish* indicates, less savoury aspects of such departures, such as rectal searches, were conducted en route, well away from public gaze. The brutal and inhumane regime they were subjected to, their future banishment from Paris, and the yellow passport they were required to carry on release made social rehabilitation of convicts extremely difficult, and the old lag's tale, told in coarse prison slang (Chapter 23), is, though fictional, no doubt not an uncommon one.

The intolerable thought of the judicially licensed act of retaliatory murder is what bulks largest in *The Last Day of a Condemned Man* and its accompanying paratexts. The guillotine was a true invention of the French Revolution, thought to be so rationally expeditious as to constitute a mercy killing. Its inventor's name was Schmitt, but the apparatus is traditionally associated with Doctor Guillotin (1738–1814), who is quoted as having recommended it to the Constituent Assembly in December 1789 with the overly enthusiastic words: 'Before you can blink, I shall cut your head off without your feeling the slightest pain'. Death-penalty abolitionists begged to differ, and Chapter 39 of the novel rehearses the argument, believed to be proven by the researches of Doctor Jean-Joseph Sue, that the posthumous sensation of pain might linger in the head and the spinal cord for several minutes.

Hugo's Preface of March 1832 added further muscle to their campaign. In it, he showed how a temporary suspension of the death penalty (to protect the ministers involved in the issue of Charles X's dictatorial ordinances, which attempted to curtail press freedom and civil liberties in July 1830) led to grisly mechanical malfunctions when guillotines were again pressed into service more than a year later. More hypocritical still was the attempt to defuse the controversy by thereafter conducting public executions at daybreak at the city gates, not, as before, on the Place de Grève (now buried under the anodyne paved expanse to be found in front of the Hôtel de Ville of Paris). It was a correct move, but for the wrong, i.e. politically expedient, reasons. Of course it was as well that the public be deprived of opportunities to indulge in self-righteous satisfaction, and not only in respect of public executions; at the time of Hugo's writing *The Last Day*, amputation of the fists of parricides and regicides, the humiliation of *exposition publique* (chaining an offender by a collar to a post as a spectacle for mockery), and the application of brand marks to felons' right shoulders, were all carried out on this square within sight of Notre-Dame cathedral. Indeed, two years later Hugo would show it as it was in 1483, and situate the hanging of Esmeralda there, in a deliberate attempt to show how little more humane society had since become. And in a novella based on the real-life killing of a prison guard, *Claude Gueux* (1832), the author imagines a riot in the centre of Troyes after poor Gueux's decapitation: 'On that very day, with the apparatus still standing unwashed in the market square, the vendors rioted over some increase in dues and nearly killed a town tax collector. What peace-loving citizens our laws do create!'

Hugo's novel is almost classical in its simplicity, and sparing in referential detail, though the odd comment locates it in an identifiable present of 1828. It is notable that an authorial artifice deprives the reader of the customary satisfaction of reading the story of events leading up to the crime. The prisoner decides to come clean, and to pen an analeptic flashback so that his daughter may one day be in a position to understand (Chapter 46), but it is then claimed either that he never had time, or that the account was mislaid. The fate he feared for the diary as a whole – 'But who is to say that after my death the wind shall not whip these papers across the muddy prison yard, or plaster them over the cracks in some gaoler's window, where slowly they will rot in the rain?' (Chapter 6) – is perhaps realised, but luckily only in the micro-cosmical aspect. Since the child Marie's mother refuses to visit, his felony would appear to have resulted from a quarrel with a mistress or a whore, indeed perhaps a crime of passion that may be held to be unpremeditated; but the jury confounds the expectations of the defence counsel. There is no suggestion of any miscarriage of justice, simply that society is barbaric in inflicting a torture which consists of letting a man gaze on the exact moment when he will die: 'What is physical pain beside its moral counterpart?' (Chapter 6)

No extraneous detail, then, was to be allowed to detract from the intellectual force of Hugo's arguments, omnipresent in the text and presented with full rhetorical force in his Preface, at the conclusion of which latter he predicted of the death penalty in general and the guillotine in particular that they 'will leave France for good and, God willing, will limp away in pain'. But would he have believed how long it would take? Certainly public executions went private for a while, only to resurface by the end of the century, when we find one described in Zola's *Paris*, as a pretext for mob hatred and frenzy. It was not until 1981 that the 'old and rickety scale of crimes and punishments' (*Claude Gueux*) was fully renovated by Robert Badinter, Minister of Justice of the incoming Socialist government, who was instrumental in fulfilling Hugo's most heartfelt wish by acting to abolish the death penalty.

— *Geoff Woollen, 2002*

The Last Day
of a Condemned Man

PREFACE

The first editions of this work, that initially did not bear its author's name, were prefaced by the following brief lines:

> There are two ways to account for the existence of this book. Either there was indeed a bundle of yellowing papers of various sizes on which were found, recorded one by one, a poor devil's last thoughts; or there was a man, a dreamer who acquainted himself with nature for the benefit of his art, a philosopher, perhaps even a poet, whose imagination gave birth to this idea, and who took it, or more likely was possessed by it, until he could only wrestle free of it by flinging it into a book.
>
> Of these two possibilities, the reader may choose the one that he prefers.

As can be seen, when the book was first published the author did not consider that the time was ripe to give full expression to his thoughts. He preferred to wait until they were understood, to see whether they would be. They were. Today, the author can reveal the political and social ideas that he wished to bring to the public's attention under this innocent and transparent literary disguise. He therefore states, and indeed publicly proclaims that *The Last Day of a Condemned Man* is nothing less than an appeal, direct or indirect as the reader wishes, for the abolition of the death penalty. What he intended to do, and what he would wish posterity to see in his work if ever it were to consider such a trifle, is not a piece of special pleading for any particular selected criminal or preferred defendant, as easy to conduct as its import will be ephemeral, but rather a general and permanent plea for all those accused in the present and the future, and this major point of law regarding human rights to be raised and pleaded as loudly as possible before society, the great court of appeal. It is the supreme veto, *abhorrescere a sanguine* ['deplore the shedding of blood'], that should exist prior to all criminal trials; it is the dark and fatal question which pulses darkly at the nub of all capital accusations beneath the triple layer of pathos in which the bloody rhetoric of the prosecution would smother it; it is, I say, the question of life and death, stripped, denuded, and laid bare of the hollow clichés of the courtroom, dragged into daylight and exposed where it deserves to be seen, where it has to remain, and in its real, true and appalling locus, not in the court but on the scaffold, not in the hands of the judge but in the executioner's.

This was his intention. Though it is hardly to be hoped for, if one day posterity were to recognise his merit in having done so, he desires no other mark of honour.

Therefore he declares and reiterates that he represents prisoners of every time, be they innocent or guilty, before all courts, all tribunals, all juries, and every form of justice. This book is addressed to whomsoever passes judgement. And so that the defence speech may be of the widest possible relevance – which is why *The Last Day of a Condemned Man* has been written as it has – he has tried everywhere to eliminate the contingent, the accidental, the particular, the special, the relative, the modifiable, the episodic, the anecdotal, the event, the proper name, and to limit himself (if indeed it be a limitation) to defending the case of any condemned man, executed on any day for any crime. It will be enough if, by the sole power of his intellect, he has delved deep enough to make a heart bleed beneath the *oes triplex* ['triple layer of armour'] of the magistrate! if he has inspired pity in those who consider themselves to be just! and if he has sufficiently penetrated the judge to succeed, now and then, in resurrecting a man!

Three years ago, when this book appeared, some people had nothing better to do than to dispute the originality of the author's inspiration. Some surmised that it was an English work, others that it was American. What misdirected curiosity it is that looks for origins thousands of miles away, and makes the water that runs down your gutter flow from the sources of the Nile! Alas! here there is no English book, and no American or Chinese one either. The author found his inspiration for *The Last Day of a Condemned Man* not in a book, for he normally looks closer to home, but where you could all find it, where indeed you may well have already (for who has not mentally rehearsed or executed *The Last Day of a Condemned Man*?), quite simply in a public place, the Place de Grève. It is from there that, as he passed by one day, he picked up the theme of death, lying in a pool of blood under the red stumps of the guillotine.

Since then, on each of the dread Thursdays of the Court of Appeal that a death sentence was proclaimed through Paris, each time that the author heard passing under his window the hoarse criers who bring spectators flocking to La Grève, each time the nagging idea returned to him, gripped him, filled his head with gendarmes, executioners, and crowds, and accompanied him hour by hour through the final sufferings of the poor man about to die: just now he is being confessed, now his hair is being cut, now his hands are being bound. The poet's poor voice was then imperiously bidden to hide nothing from a society that does business while this monstrous business is being transacted; he was pressured, pushed, and shaken; lines of poetry were ripped from his brain, if he was busy rhyming them, and killed whilst barely formed; all his work was interrupted or sabotaged; he was invaded, obsessed, and under siege. It was like a torment that began at daybreak and which lasted, like that of the wretched man who was being tortured at the same time, until *four o'clock*. Only then, when the *ponens caput expiravit* ['laying down his head, he died'] had been told by the gloomy voice of the clock, could the author breathe again and regain some peace of mind. Until at last, on the day following the execution of Ulbach[1], if memory serves, he began to write this book. Since then, he has felt relief. When one of those public crimes that are called judicial executions has been committed, his conscience has declared him innocent of complicity; and he has no longer felt his forehead wetted by a drop of blood that spatters from La Grève on to the heads of all members of the social community.

But this is not enough. It is good to wash one's hands, but to prevent blood from being spilled on them would be better.

Consequently he holds no mission to be higher, more sacred or deserving than to campaign for the abolition of the death penalty.

So it is that he expresses the most heartfelt support for the wishes and efforts of men of goodwill from all nations who have been working for years to fell the gallows tree, the only one that revolutions do not uproot. It is with pride that this insignificant man now aims his axe into the widening notch marked sixty-six years ago by Beccaria on the old gibbet that has towered for so many centuries over Christendom.

As we said above, the scaffold is the only construction that revolutions do not demolish. For rarely are revolutions innocent of human blood and, since they occur in order to dock, lop, and pollard society, the death penalty is one of the pruning blades they surrender most unwillingly.

We will allow, however, that if ever a revolution appeared worthy and capable of abolishing the death penalty, it was the July Revolution. The time seemed ripe for the most merciful popular movement of modern times to strike out the barbarous penal statutes of Louis XI, Richelieu, and Robespierre, and to write the inviolability of human life into the legal code. 1830 deserved to smash the blade of '93.

And this much we hoped for a while. In August 1830 there was so much altruism and pity in the air, the masses were imbued with such a spirit of gentleness and civilisation, and hearts were so uplifted by the prospect of a glorious future, that we thought that the death penalty had been immediately and automatically abolished by tacit and unanimous consent, like the rest of the abuses that had plagued us. The people had just made a bonfire of the remnants of the *ancien régime*. This was the bloody remnant, and we believed it to be in the pile. We thought it had been burned along with the others. And for some weeks, in confident trust, our hope for the future was that life would be as inviolate as liberty.

What is more, scarce two months had gone by when an attempt was made to turn the sublime Utopia of Cesare Bonesana[2] into a legal reality.

Unfortunately, this attempt was naive, clumsy, almost hypocritical, and made for reasons that had little to do with the common good.

6

In October 1830, it will be remembered, a few days after having rejected the proposal to bury Napoleon under the column, the whole Chamber began to cry and to lament. The question of the death penalty was put on the agenda, in what context we shall state presently, and it seemed that the bowels of all these legislators were suddenly and miraculously moved by mercy. Speakers fell over themselves to intervene, to groan, to lift up their hands to heaven. The death penalty, dear God! how dreadful! Some old state prosecutor, whose hair had turned white during his years dressed in red, who all his life had eaten the blood-soaked bread his indictments had earned him, suddenly donned an expression of commiseration and swore blind that he was outraged by the guillotine. For two days, a never-ending stream of demagogues-cum-mourners were called to speak. It was a general lamentation, a funeral dirge, a concert of gloomy psalms, a *Super flumina Babylonis*, a *Stabat mater dolorosa*, a great choral symphony in C, performed by the complete orchestra of orators sitting on the front benches of the Chamber, who make such fine music on the historic days. To the bass of one responded the falsetto of another. Nothing was lacking. A more pathetic and heart-rending sight you never did see. The all-night sitting, in particular, was as tender, benevolent, and tear-jerking as the denouement of a La Chaussée play. The eyes of the bemused spectators in the gallery were moist.[*]

So what was it all about? The abolition of the death penalty?

Yes and no.

This is what it was all about:

Four men of the world, four men who were well connected in society, the kind of men one may have met in a salon, and with whom one may have exchanged a few words of conventional politeness, four of these men, then, had attempted in the higher reaches of political power one of the bold coups that Bacon calls

* *Hugo's note*: We do not wish to heap the same degree of scorn on *everything* that was said at that time in the Chamber. Now and then, some fine and noble words were spoken. Like everybody else, we applauded the grave simplicity of Monsieur de Lafayette's speech and, in another register, Monsieur de Villemain's remarkable improvisation.

crimes, and Machiavelli, *enterprises*. Now be it a crime or an enterprise, the even-handed harshness of justice punishes it by death. So, the four unfortunate men were held prisoner, the law's captives, guarded by three hundred tricolour plumes beneath the fine vaults of Vincennes[3]. What was to be done, and how? Please understand that it is not possible to dispatch in a cart bound for La Grève, ignobly tied up with thick ropes, rubbing shoulders with that civil servant who may not even be named, four men like you and me, four *men of the world*! Why, at the very least the guillotine would have to be built of mahogany!

But wait! Why not just abolish the death penalty?

Whereupon the Chamber got to work.

Observe, gentlemen, that only yesterday you held abolition to be Utopian, theoretical, a dream, madness, poetic fantasy. Observe that it is not the first time that we have tried to draw your attention to the cart, the thick ropes, and the infernal scarlet machine, so that we find it strange that the hideousness of the apparatus strikes you suddenly now.

Well, so what? It is not for your precious sake, you common people, that we are abolishing the death penalty, but for ourselves, as deputies who may become ministers. We do not wish Guillotin's apparatus to bite into the upper classes. We shall break it. All the better if that suits everybody, but we thought only of ourselves. Ucalegon's is burning[4], and we must put out the fire. Quick, dismiss the executioner and strike the statute from the code.

Thus a taint of selfishness can creep into and adulterate the best social purposes. It is the black streak in white marble, running right through, surfacing everywhere you place the chisel. Your statue will need to be carved again.

Of course, as should hardly need stressing, we are not of the number that called for the heads of the four ministers. Once these wretches had been arrested, the outrage and wrath that their coup had provoked gave way, in us as in everybody else, to deep pity. We thought of the prejudices in which some of them were steeped by their upbringing, of the weak brain of their leader, who had gone prematurely grey in the dank shadows of state prisons, of the fatal obligations of their common position, of the impossibility of braking on the steep slope that royalty had galloped headlong down on 8 August 1829, of the hitherto underestimated influence of the King, and particularly of the dignity that one of them spread like a red robe over their misfortune. We can be counted among those who sincerely wished for their lives to be spared, and who were ready to make sacrifices to achieve this. If ever the impossible had happened and their scaffold had been erected one day on the Place de Grève, we are convinced, and if it is an illusion let us remain under it, yes, convinced that there would have been an uprising to demolish it, and this writer would have been part of this just revolt. For it must also be said that, in times of social crisis, of all death penalties the political is the most vile, dreadful, and noxious, and the most necessary to eradicate. The guillotine for this puts down its roots in the cobbles, but soon its shoots are springing up from the ground all over.

In times of revolution, beware of the first head that falls. It whets the people's appetite.

Therefore we were personally in agreement with those who wished to spare the lives of the four ministers, in entire agreement for both humanitarian and political reasons. Yet we would have preferred the Chamber to choose another time to seek the abolition of the death penalty.

Let us suppose that so highly desirable an abolition had been proposed, not for four ministers who had fallen from the Tuileries to Vincennes, but for any common thief, for one of those wretches whom you hardly look at when they pass you by in the street, to whom you do not speak and whose grubby contact you instinctively avoid; an unfortunate who in childhood ran ragged and barefoot through the mud of the squares, shivering in winter on the embankment, warming himself in the steam rising from Monsieur Véfour's kitchens, where you dine, occasionally spotting a crust on the rubbish heap and wiping it down before eating it, or spending the whole day raking the gutter with a nail in the hope of finding a farthing; with no entertainment but the free show on the King's birthday and the Grève executions, which are another free show;

poor devils who are driven by hunger to theft, and from theft down the slippery slope; dispossessed children of a heartless society, that the house of correction takes at twelve, the convict prison at eighteen, and the scaffold at forty; hopeless wretches whom you could have made good, respectable, and useful in a school or a workshop, but have no earthly idea what to do with beyond dumping them, like an unwanted burden, into the red-anthill of Toulon or the walled cemetery of Clamart, taking their lives after stealing their liberty. Then if for one of these men you had proposed the abolition of the death penalty, why, yes! that session would have been truly worthy, great, sacred, majestic, and deserving of profound respect. Since the time that the venerable fathers of Trent invited heretics to the Council in the name of the bowels of God, *Per viscera Dei*, and in the hope of their conversion, *quoniam sancta synodus sperat haereticorum conversionem*, never would a body of men have presented to the world a more sublime, distinguished, and merciful sight. It has always been a mark of the truly noble and the truly great that they are mindful of the humble and weak. It would be admirable for a council of Brahmins to take up the cause of the pariah. And here, the cause of the pariah was that of the people. In abolishing the death penalty for their sake, and before such time as you had a personal axe to grind, you would have accomplished not only a political, but a social act.

But by your attempt to abolish it not for its own sake, but to save four wretched ministers caught red-handed in a coup d'état, you did not even achieve a political objective!

And what happened? Because you were not sincere, suspicion was aroused. When the people saw trickery was afoot, they turned against the entire proposal and, almost unbelievably, threw their weight behind a death penalty which bears down only on them. Your bungling brought them to this. By approaching the issue crabwise, in this indirect and insincere fashion, you have jeopardised it for a long time to come. You were poor players in a farce, and rightly booed for it.

Yet some there were who had been misguided enough to take this farce seriously. Immediately after the great debate, a Keeper of the Seals of integrity issued to king's attorneys the order indefinitely to suspend all capital executions. The opponents of the death penalty breathed again. But their delusion was short-lived.

The trial of the ministers was concluded. Some verdict or other was pronounced. The four lives were spared, and the fortress of Ham chosen as a compromise between death and liberty. Once these various arrangements had been made, all fear was banished from the minds of the leaders of state, and along with fear, all humanity. There was no further talk of abolishing the supreme penalty; and as soon as they no longer required to be taken in vain, Utopia returned to being Utopian, theory to being theoretical, and poetry to being poetic.

Yet there remained in the prisons a handful of condemned common criminals, who had been taking exercise in the yards for five or six months, breathing the fresh air, their minds at ease for the future, their lives guaranteed, and taking this suspended sentence to be their pardon. Wait just a moment, though.

In truth, the executioner had been terrified. The day he had heard our lawgivers speak of humanity, philanthropy, and progress, he thought that he was done for. The wretched man had hidden out of sight beneath his guillotine, as out of his element beneath the sun of July as a night bird in daylight, hoping to be overlooked, with his fingers in his ears and holding his breath. He had not been seen for six months. He gave no sign of life. Yet gradually he had taken comfort in the darkness. Bending his ear in the direction of the Chambers, he had not heard his name spoken, or any more of the noble, ringing words that had given him such a fright. No more tub-thumping orations on the *Treatise on Crimes and Punishments*. Quite other issues were being discussed, weightier social ones, the creation of a country road, a subsidy for the Opéra-Comique, or the hundred thousand francs needing to be bled from an inflated budget of fifteen hundred million. Nobody gave a thought to him, the head-cutter. Whereupon the man calmed down, stuck his head out of his hole and looked all round: he took one step, then another, like a mouse from somewhere in La Fontaine, then he dared to come right out from beneath his scaffold, climbed up on to it, and mended, restored, and polished it lovingly. Next he tried it out, making it shine and rewaxing the rusty track that was gummed up through lack of use; and suddenly he was seen to spin round, grab the hair of a prisoner chosen at random from those who believed that their lives were spared, pull him over, strip him, strap and buckle him, and the executions began all over again.

All gruesome to relate, but historically true.

Yes, a suspended sentence of six months was granted to hapless captives whose torment was sadistically heightened by granting them a new lease of life; then, without rhyme or reason, without the reason being fully known, *as was their whim*, one fine day the suspension was revoked and once more these human creatures were subjected to the brutal, systematic fellings. Great God! I ask you, what harm did it do us if these men lived? Is there not air enough in France for all to breathe?

And if some insignificant chancery clerk, to whom it hardly mattered either way, rose from his chair, saying, 'Right! the death penalty is no longer a sensitive issue. We can begin to guillotine again!', then something abhorrent must have happened to the heart of that man.

Moreover, let it be clearly understood that executions have never been carried out with more ferocity than since the July suspension was revoked, and never have tales from La Grève been more horrifying or made the death penalty more deserving of detestation, its increased barbarity heaping deserved shame on men who have reinstated the code of blood. May they be punished by their own handiwork: it would be well done.

Two or three examples should be given of the appalling and sacrilegious nature of some executions. Wives of king's attorneys have to be upset. Sometimes a woman has a conscience.

In the south, at the end of September last, we are not quite certain of the place, the day, or the name of the victim, but shall produce them if the incident is disputed, and we believe it was Pamiers, at the end of September, then, a man was sent for in prison, where he was peacefully playing cards. He was told that he would die in two hours, at which he shuddered uncontrollably; for, six months after having been forgotten, he was no longer prepared for death. He was shaved, shorn, bound, and shriven; then, flanked by four gendarmes, he was pushed on a barrow through the crowd to the place of execution. Pure routine so far; that's how it's done. When he reached the scaffold, the executioner took over from the priest, tied him in place on the swinging-plank, *put him in the oven*, to use the slang expression, and activated the blade. The heavy metal triangle jerked stickily into motion, jolted downwards between the grooves, and – prepare yourselves for the unthinkable – sliced into the man without killing him. The man let out a blood-curdling cry. The executioner was flustered, wound the blade back up and released it again. The blade bit into the neck of the condemned man once more, but did not sever it. The victim howled, and the crowd with him. The executioner raised the blade once again, hoping for third time lucky. Unfortunately not: the third stroke caused a third stream of blood to spurt from the condemned man's neck, but the head did not fall. Let us curtail this: the blade rose and fell five times, five times it cut into the man, and five times he howled beneath the blow and shook his living head, begging for mercy! The people were outraged, picked up stones, and meted out their own justice on the unfortunate executioner. The headsman dived down beneath the guillotine and crouched there behind the protection of the police horses. But you have not heard the end of it. Alone now on the scaffold, the victim had stood up on the platform, a gruesome, blood-soaked sight, and holding up his half-severed head which was dangling on his shoulder, he weakly begged to be set free. The crowd, filled with pity, was about to push past the gendarmes and come to the assistance of a wretch who had paid the death penalty five times over. Just then, an executioner's assistant, a young man of twenty, climbed on to the scaffold, told the victim to turn to have his bonds undone and, seizing the opportunity offered by a dying man who trusted him, jumped on his back and began to hack away at what remained of his neck with some butcher's knife. It happened. It was seen to happen. Deny it if you dare.

According to the law's provision, a judge must have witnessed this execution! A sign from him would have put a stop to it. So what was this man doing, in his comfortable carriage, while another man was being butchered? What distracted this scourge of killers while killing was being done in broad daylight, before his very eyes, beneath his horses' nostrils, close to his carriage window?

But the judge was not brought to trial! And the executioner was not brought to trial! And there has been no judicial enquiry into this monstrous desecration of every human law in dealing with the sacred person of one of God's creatures!

In the seventeenth century, the time of Richelieu and Christophe Fouquet that marked the dark ages of the criminal code, when Monsieur de Chalais was executed in the presence of Le Bouffay de Nantes by a clumsy soldier who, instead of a clean sword-cut, administered thirty-four blows of a cooper's adze[*5], the parliament was shamed into finding this procedure irregular. An enquiry and a trial were held, and though Richelieu was not punished, at least the soldier was. Unjust, no doubt, but indicative of some desire for justice.

But here there was nothing. The event took place after July, at a time of law-abiding behaviour and progress, a year after the Chamber's well-publicised qualms of conscience over the death penalty. Well, it went entirely unobserved. The Paris newspapers treated it as though it were apocryphal. Nobody was reprimanded. All that came out was that the guillotine had been deliberately sabotaged by somebody *who wished to discredit the high executioner*. An assistant dismissed by him had taken his revenge by playing this practical joke.

Very well, then, it was no more than a joke. But let us continue.

In Dijon, three months ago, a woman was led out to pay the penalty. (A woman!) Once again Doctor Guillotin's blade performed poorly. The head was not entirely severed. So the executioner's helpers all grabbed hold of the woman's feet, pulling and jerking while the hapless woman screamed, and in this way they

* *Hugo's note*: La Porte says twenty-two, but Aubrey says thirty-four. Monsieur de Chalais cried out until the twentieth.

14

succeeded in ripping the head clean away from the body.

In Paris, we are back to the days of secret executions. Since July they no longer dare to cut off heads on the Place de Grève, being afraid and cowardly, so this is what they do. Recently, a condemned prisoner, by the name of Désandrieux, I believe, was taken from Bicêtre; he was put into a sort of basket on two wheels with no windows, and bolted and padlocked in; then, with a gendarme in front and one behind, moving quietly so as to attract no crowd, they delivered the consignment to the deserted city limits at the Barrière Saint-Jacques. When they got there, at eight in the morning just after daybreak, a brand new guillotine was standing there, and the only spectators were a dozen boys standing on the stone heaps around this unscheduled construction; the man swiftly was pulled from the basket, and before he was allowed to draw breath, furtively, stealthily, and shamefully they whipped off his head. And this is called a solemn and public manifestation of high justice. Ignoble farce!

How, then, does the King's justice interpret the word civilisation? How low have we sunk? Is justice reduced to bluff and deception? Is the law dependent on expedients? How monstrous!

Is a condemned man such a fearsome creature that society needs to deal with him with such sly treachery as this?

Yet fairness requires us to say that the execution was not entirely secret. That morning the customary announcement was made and hawked in the public places of Paris. It seems that there are people who make a living from its sale. Do you follow? An unfortunate man's crime, his punishment, his tortures, and his final moments are turned into a commodity, a paper that is sold for a sou. Could anything be more hideous than this coin enslimed by blood? Who would stoop to pick it up?

We have cited enough examples, too many in fact. But is all this not horrific? What have you got to say in favour of the death penalty?

We ask this question seriously, and in order to receive an answer; we ask it of the criminal jurists, and not of prolix men of letters. We know that there are some who take the desirability of the death penalty, like any other topic, as an opportunity to be controversial. Others support the death penalty only because of their aversion to someone or other who happens to be an opponent of it. For such, it can be a near-literary pretext, a matter of person-alities or of names. Among the latter are the envious satellites who are as often to be found around legal experts as in the retinue of great artists. The Joseph Grippas are as inseparable from the Filangieri as the Torregiani are from Michelangelo, and the Scudérys from the Corneilles.

Not to these do we speak, but to the men of law proper, to the logicians, to the rational thinkers, to those who love the death penalty for itself, for its beauty, its mercy, and its elegance.

Could these men please speak in justification of it?

Those who judge and condemn claim the death penalty to be necessary, first, 'because a member of the social community must be banished from it if he has already done damage and may do so again'. If that were all, life imprisonment would suffice: why death? You counter this, perhaps, by saying that people escape from prison. Then keep better watch over them. If you do not believe iron bars to be strong enough, how come you keep wild animals in cages?

No executioner is required when the gaoler is competent.

But secondly, you say, 'society must exact vengeance, and society must punish'. Wrong on both counts. Vengeance comes from the individual, and punishment from God.

Society is poised between the two. Punishment is too far above, and vengeance too far beneath it. Nothing so great or so petty can be appropriate. We must not 'strike in vengeance' but *improve by correction*. Turn the criminologists' dictum round to this and it will be fully understood and supported.

But there is a third and final argument, the theory of exemplary justice: 'We must make an example! The sight of the fate reserved for criminals must terrify those who might be tempted to act in the same way!' This is more or less the exact wording of the sempiternal theme on which all indictments pronounced in the five hundred law courts of France are but louder or softer variations.

Well, first of all, we fail to see the point of making an example. We contend that public punishments do not produce the desired effect. Far from edifying the common people, they deprave them and destroy in them all finer feelings, and consequently all civic virtue. There exists proof abundant of this, but to cite it would encumber our argument. One incident taken from a thousand of its kind may be mentioned because it occurred the most recently, ten days before the time of writing. At Saint-Pol, straight after the execution of an arsonist called Louis Camus, a masked gang began to dance around the still-reeking scaffold. Make an example, then! and Mardi Gras revellers laugh in your face!

So that if, despite evidence to the contrary, you remain attached to your banal theory of the example, then transport us back to the sixteenth century, be truly terrifying, give us the whole range of tortures, give us Farinacius[6], give us the torturers-in-chief, give us the gibbet, the wheel, the stake, skinning, cropping, drawing, the pit for burial alive, the pot for boiling alive. Bring back the executioner's grisly stall, with its regular deliveries of human flesh, as one more shop on the public places of Paris. Bring back Mont-faucon, with its sixteen pillars of stone, its massive foundations, its caves full of bones, its beams, its hooks, its chains, its skewered skeletons, its white mound speckled with crows, its secondary gibbets, and the stench of corpses that gusts in on the north-east wind over the whole of the Faubourg du Temple. Yes, reinstate in its original splendour the Paris executioner's gigantic glory hole. Why not, indeed? An example will be made on a truly grand scale. The death penalty as it really ought to be. Punishment that truly fits the crime. A thing of horror, but a thing of terror.

Or else, do as they do in England. In shopkeeper England, a smuggler arrested on the Dover coast is hanged *as an example*, and *as an example* he is left dangling from the gallows; but, as bad weather could rot the corpse, it is carefully wrapped in tarred cloth so that it will need to be replaced less often. O frugal country, that tars its hanged bodies!

Yet there is some logic to this. It is the most humane way to interpret the theory of exemplary justice.

But as for you, do you seriously claim to teach by example when you cravenly slit the throat of some poor man at the loneliest spot on the outer boulevards? There is something to be said for La Grève, in broad daylight, but the Barrière Saint-Jacques! and at eight in the morning! Who walks there? Who goes near there? An example for whose benefit? Perhaps for the trees that line the boulevard.

Do you not see that your public executions are performed in stealth? Do you not see that you are hiding? That you are afraid and ashamed of your handiwork? That with spinelessness and lack of conviction you mumble your *discite justitiam moniti* ['Learn by this example what justice means']? That deep down you are unconvinced, hesitating to speak, unsure of whether you are right, touched by the all-pervading scepticism, routinely cutting off heads with little inkling of what you are doing? Do you not feel in your bones that, to put it mildly, you lack the moral and social appetite for the errand of blood that your veteran predecessors in parliament would go on with a clear conscience? At night, do your heads not toss on the pillow far more violently than theirs? Others before you ordered capital executions, but they believed themselves to be in the right, acting justly for the common good. Jouvenel des Ursins was sure he was a judge; Élie de Thorette was sure he was a judge; even Laubardemont, La Reynie, and Laffemas were sure that they were judges; but you, in your heart of hearts, cannot quite be sure that you are not murderers!

You prefer the Barrière Saint-Jacques to La Grève, a desert to a crowd, and twilight to day. What you do you no longer do decisively. You are hiding, I tell you!

So all your reasons for the death penalty have been refuted. And all your three-part legal syllogisms dismantled, all these snatches of indictments swept away and reduced to ashes. The least hint of logic is fatal to all sophistries.

Therefore let the King's justice no longer expect from us, as jurors and as men, that we will give it heads in response to its wheedling pleas for examples to be made, society protected, and public morality preserved. What windy rhetoric and empty figures of speech! The merest prick, and this verbiage is punctured. At the root of their ingratiating discourse you will find only hardness of heart, cruelty, barbarism, boot-licking and fee-grubbing. Be silent you mandarins! Beneath the silken paw of the judge, the claws of the executioner can be felt.

It is difficult to think calmly of what being a king's attorney entails. This man earns his living by sending others to their dying. He'll see you get your part in the Place de Grève performance. Not only this, he is a gentleman who prides himself on his style and his learning, who is a fine orator, at least in his own estimation, who can quote a couple of Latin verses for effect before requiring the death penalty, who hams up his part, who projects his pathetic ego while others' lives are at stake, who has role models whom he despairs of ever emulating, his Bellart and his Marchangy, as one poet aspires to be Racine, and another to be Boileau. In the court proceedings, his role and his calling are to be on the side of the guillotine. His indictment is his contribution to literature, decked out with metaphors and scented with quotations, for the court to admire and the ladies to enjoy. He has his stock of commonplaces that still sound original in the provinces, his refinements of diction, and his crafted, writerly elegance. He detests blunt terminology almost as much as the disciples of our tragic poet, Delille. There is no danger of him calling a spade a spade. The very thought of it! For every idea that would shock you in its unvarnished form, he has a complete costume change of epithets and adjectives. He makes Monsieur Samson quite presentable. He drapes gauze over the guillotine blade. He draws a veil over the swinging-plank. He wraps the bloody basket in euphemisms, so that you no longer know what it is, if not rose-tinted and respectable. Can you not see him at night, in his study, slowly and lovingly polishing the fiery speech that will erect a guillotine in six weeks' time? Do you not see him, sweating blood to entrap the head of the accused in the most damning article of the Code? Can you not see him hacking at the neck of a wretch with a blunt instrument of law? Do you not observe how a hotchpotch of figures and metaphors can be steeped in the venom of two or three vicious citations until out of them can slowly be squeezed the death of a man? Is it not true that, as he writes, in the shadow beneath his table the executioner must lie crouched at his feet, so that he raises his pen from time to time and says to him, like a master to his dog, 'Down, boy, down! you'll get your bone!'

And in private life, of course, this king's servant may be a respectable man, a good father, good son, good husband, and good friend, as we find written over all the tombstones of Père-Lachaise.

May the day not be far removed when the law will abolish these dismal professions. Surely the very air of our civilisation will sooner or later erode the death penalty.

One is sometimes tempted to believe that the partisans of the death penalty have not fully considered what it represents. Yet weigh in the balance against any crime you care to name the outrageous right claimed by society to take away what it has not given, of all the irreparable punishments the most irreparable!

There are but two alternatives:

Either the man you punish has no family, no relatives, no ties that bind in this world. In which case he has received no schooling, no education, no attention has been paid to his heart or his mind; therefore by what right do you kill this hapless orphan? You punish him because he has been dragged up, untrained and unsupported! The solitude in which you left him is held against him! You hold his misfortune to be a crime! Nobody taught him to know right from wrong. This man is ignorant. His destiny is the culprit, and not he. You punish an innocent man.

Or else the man has a family; in which case, do you believe that to slit his throat wounds him alone? and that his father, his mother, and his children will not also shed blood? Of course they will: in killing him, you strike the head from his entire family. And once again, you punish innocents.

O blind and clumsy sanctions, which one way or the other strike at the innocent!

If the guilty man has a family, why not lock him up? In his imprisonment he can still work for his dependants. But how will he support them from beyond the grave? And can you think without flinching of what will become of the little boys and little girls who are deprived of their father, their very daily bread? Are you somehow expecting the family's men to end up in prison in fifteen years, and the women in low dance halls? O innocent victims!

In the colonies, when a slave is sentenced to death his owner receives a thousand francs in compensation. So you reimburse the master, but fail to compensate the family! For here, too, do you not take a man from those who own him? Is he not, to a more sacred degree than the slave to his master, his father's property, his wife's possession and his children's chattel?

Your law already stands convicted of murder; and now, of theft.

One more thing: do you care for the soul of this man? Do you know how it fares? Do you rest easy in dispatching it so speedily? Formerly, at least, the people had a degree of faith; at the final moment, the breath of religion that moved through the air could soften the most hardened criminal; a victim was also a penitent; religion opened up a world to him just as society was rejecting him from another; every soul could apprehend God; the scaffold was but a gateway to heaven. But what confidence can you have in the scaffold now that people at large do not believe? now that all religions are attacked by dry rot, like those old hulks that may once have discovered new worlds, only to lie mouldering in our ports? now that little children thumb their noses at God? By what right do you send the benighted souls of your condemned, souls that are the handiwork of Voltaire and Monsieur Pigault-Lebrun, hurtling towards a destination that you yourselves cannot be sure of? You hand them over to the prison chaplain, a worthy old gentleman no doubt; but does he believe, and can he convert? What if his blessed errand is performed as though it were a dreary task? Can this fellow who stands next to the executioner in the cart be seriously taken for a priest? As a writer of courage and talent has already stated: *How terrible to have done away with the confessor and kept the executioner!*

No doubt these reasons will be found 'emotive' by the blasé among you whose logic is purely cerebral. But to our mind they are the most valid. We are often led by the reasons of the heart, and not the reasons of the head. Besides, it should not be forgotten that the two varieties support one another. The *Treatise on Crimes* has been grafted onto the stock of *The Spirit of Laws*. Montesquieu is the father of Beccaria.

Reason is on our side, feeling is on our side, experience is on our side. In states worthy of the name, in which the death penalty has been abolished, the total of capital crimes is in yearly decline. Weigh this carefully.

Yet we do not call at this time for sudden and complete abolition of the death penalty, the path down which the Chamber of Deputies had so irresponsibly gone; rather, we should prefer it to be for an experimental period, accompanied by every safeguard, and handled with the greatest sensitivity. Nor are we campaigning simply for the abolition of the death penalty, but for a complete review of sentencing policy from top to bottom, from confinement through to decapitation, and time is necessary if such an undertaking is properly to be carried out. We hope in other writings to give more detailed expression to the guiding principles that we deem appropriate. But, as well as calling for the remission of the death sentence in cases of counterfeiting, arson, aggravated burglary, and the like, we request with immediate effect in all capital cases the judge be required to put to the jury the following question: *Was the accused motivated by passion or self-interest?* and that if the jury replies: *by passion*, then there should be no death sentence. Some repellent executions at least could thus be spared us. Ulbach's and Debacker's lives would not be forfeit. Othello would not be guillotined.

Let us be clear that the dilemma of the death penalty grows more acute with every passing day. Soon, society as a whole will find as we do.

And the most obdurate penologists would do well to heed that capital punishment has been in decline for a century. It has become almost merciful. A sign of senility. A sign of weakness. A sign of imminent demise. Torture has disappeared. The wheel has disappeared. The gibbet has disappeared. Strange as it may seem, the guillotine constituted progress.

Monsieur Guillotin was a philanthropist.

Yes, the bloodthirsty, sabre-toothed Themis of Farinacius and Le Vouglans, of Delancre and Isaac Loisel, of d'Oppède and of Machault[7] is failing visibly. She is wasting away. Dying.

For La Grève has already had enough. La Grève is mending her ways. The blood-swigging old crone behaved well in July. She now wants to live a better life, and to remain worthy of her recent good deed. Having lent her body to all the executions of the last three hundred years, she has now gone all coy. She is ashamed of her former calling. She wants to lose her bad name. She disowns the executioner. She is washing down her cobblestones.

At the time of writing, the death penalty takes place outside the walls of Paris. Make no mistake, to leave Paris is to leave civilisation behind.

So all the omens are in our favour. It seems, too, as though signs of unwillingness and refusal are being shown by that ghastly machine, the monster of wood and iron that is to Guillotin what Galatea was to Pygmalion[8]. From one point of view, the appalling executions described above promise wonderfully well. The guillotine procrastinates. It is no longer reliable. The ramshackle props that support the death penalty are quivering.

It is our devout hope that the infamous machine will leave France for good and, God willing, will limp away in pain, for we shall endeavour to deal it some good blows first.

Let it go where it will and seek hospitality from some uncivilised race, though not in progressive Turkey or from savage tribes, for they would have no part of it[*]; let it go further still down the ladder of civilisation, perhaps to Spain or to Russia.

The social fabric of the past reposed on three pillars: the priest, the king, and the executioner. A long time ago, a voice was heard to say: *The gods are departing!* Recently, another voice rang out, crying: *The kings are departing!* It is time now for a third voice to rise and proclaim: *The executioner is departing!*

Thus, stone by stone, the old society will have fallen; thus Providence will have completed the destruction of the past.

* *Hugo's note*: The 'parliament' of Tahiti recently abolished the death penalty.

To those who lamented the passing of the gods, it could be said: God remains. To those who would weep for the passing of the executioner, nothing can be said.

But do not believe that law and order will be banished with the executioner. The roof of the society of the future will not collapse if this grisly keystone is removed. Civilisation is nothing other than a series of successive transformations. What therefore is in store for us, if not a transformation of penal law? The merciful precepts of Christ will at last suffuse the Code, and it will glow with their radiance. Crime will be considered an illness, with its own doctors to replace your judges, and its hospitals to replace your prisons. Liberty shall be equated with health. Ointments and oil shall be applied to limbs that were once shackled and branded. Infirmities that once were scourged with anger shall now be bathed with love. The cross in place of the gallows: sublime, and yet so simple.

— Victor Hugo, 15 March 1832

Condemned to death!

For five weeks now I have lived with this thought, forever alone and petrified in its presence, forever bent beneath the burden of it!

Once upon a time, for now it seems like years ago rather than weeks, I was a man like any other. I had as many thoughts as there were days, hours, and minutes. My brain was fresh, fertile, full of delightful fancies, and took pleasure in running them by me in random, unceasing succession, embroidering with infinite tapestries the rough and flimsy stuff of life. There were young women and splendid bishops' robes, battles won, theatres brimming with noise and light, and more young women, with whom I walked at night under the spreading branches of the chestnut trees. My imagination ran riot; my thoughts knew no bounds. I was free.

Now I am a captive. My body is fettered in a cell, my brain imprisoned in a fixed idea, and dreadful, bloody, and merciless it is! I now have but one thought, a lone conviction and a single certainty: that I am condemned to death!

Try as I will, this hellish thought will not leave me, like a leaden ghost at my elbow that imperiously banishes all other preoccupations, reflects my wretchedness back at me, and shakes me in its icy grasp when I wish to turn my head away or close my eyes. It assumes all the guises in which my mind seeks refuge, mingles in grim chorus with all the words spoken to me, stands by me as I press against the hateful bars of my cell, nags me during my waking hours, watches over my fitful sleep, and recurs in my dreams in the shape of a knife.

I have just been jolted awake, pursued by this thought but telling myself, 'It was only a dream!' If only it were! For long before my heavy lids have opened wide enough to see this fatal obsession writ large in the grim reality of my surroundings, which are the damp, clammy flags of my cell, the dim beam of my night-light, the coarse weave of my garments, the brooding face of the sentry with his ammunition pouch dully glinting through the bars, already it seems that a voice has whispered in my ear, 'Condemned to death!'

It was one fine morning in August.

Three days before my trial had begun; for three days now my name and my crime had alerted a flock of spectators, who swooped down on the benches of the court like crows sighting a corpse; and for three days the surreal pageant of judges, witnesses, defence, and prosecution had ebbed and flowed before me, now grotesque, now bloody, but always dark and threatening. On the first two nights anxiety and panic stopped me from sleeping a wink, but by the third I had succumbed to tedium and tiredness. At midnight, while the jury were still deliberating, I had been brought back to the straw of my cell and fell at once fast asleep, into the sleep of forgetfulness – my first hours of repose for a good many days.

At the deepest point of my deep slumber, they came and woke me again. This time neither the heavy tread of the warder's hobnailed boots, the jingling of his bunch of keys, nor the harsh screech of the bolts being drawn back could rouse me from my torpor before his rough hand was on my arm, and his rough voice barking in my ear, 'On your feet!' I opened my eyes, and sat up in terror. At that moment, through the narrow window set high on my cell wall, I saw on the ceiling of the corridor that ran outside, which was the nearest I got to seeing the sky, the yellow glow that eyes accustomed to prison darkness know unfailingly to be the sun. I love the sun.

'Fine day,' I said to the gaoler.

He was silent for a moment, as though not certain that this warranted a reply, then forced himself gruffly to mumble, 'I suppose so.'

I made no movement, my mind still half asleep, with a smile on my lips as I gazed on the gentle, golden reflection that dappled the ceiling. 'What a fine day,' I repeated.

'Yes,' replied the man, 'but they are waiting for you.'

These few words, like the cobweb that arrests an insect in full flight, dumped me unceremoniously into the real world. In a sudden flash of recognition I saw the dingy courtroom, the sickle-shaped judges' bench draped in bloody rags, the three rows of bovine witnesses, the two gendarmes sitting at either side of my bench, the black gowns tossing, the heads of the crowd dancing in the dim light at the back, and swivelling to fix itself upon me, the relentless gaze of those twelve jurors who had sat up while I slept!

I got up; my teeth were chattering, my trembling hands groped vainly for my clothes, and my legs felt weak. I took one step and stumbled, like a porter bent double beneath his burden. Nevertheless, I followed the gaoler.

The two gendarmes were waiting for me at the door of the cell. They put the handcuffs on me. There was an intricate little lock, and they did it up with care. I offered no resistance: what was one cog in a bigger mechanism?

We crossed an inner courtyard. The chill morning air revived me. I raised my head: the sky was blue and the warm rays of the sun, bisected by the tall chimneys, cut out jagged swathes of light high on the dismal walls of the prison. It was indeed a fine day.

We climbed a spiral staircase and went down a corridor, a second and then a third. A low door opened, and a hot and noisy blast of air struck me in the face: it was the breath of the crowd gathered in the courtroom, which I entered.

As I came into view, there was a rustle of arms and voices, the noise of seats being moved and partitions creaking. While I walked the whole length of the room, between two crowds of spectators held back by soldiers, I felt like the nodal point to which were connected the nerves that operated all those vacant faces and craning necks.

Just then I noticed that I had no leg-irons on, but had no idea when or where they had been removed.

Deep silence then fell. I had reached my place. As the crowd's din subsided, so too did the din in my head. Suddenly I grasped with clarity what had hitherto been only dimly apprehended: the moment of truth had come, and I was there to be sentenced.

Strangely enough, this idea came to me in a way that inspired no fear. The windows were open, with air and noise flooding freely in from the city streets; the courtroom was gaily lit as if for a wedding; the sun's bright rays cast random patterns from the leaded panes, here elongated on the floor, there spread across the tables, now bent where two walls met, and each shining pane projected a hazy golden prism that hovered in the air.

At the far end of the room the judges looked satisfied, no doubt relieved that it would soon be over. The president's face, lit gently by the gleam from a window-pane, looked calm and kindly, and a young barrister was toying with his jabot as he chatted almost jovially with a pretty lady in a pink hat, who occupied a privileged position behind him.

Only the jurors seemed pale and drawn, but were clearly weary from having been up all night. Some were yawning. There was no indication from their expressions that they had just delivered a verdict of death, and I discerned no more in the faces of these good men and true than a desperate longing for sleep.

Opposite me, a window had been thrown wide open. I could hear flower-girls laughing on the river embankment, and on the stone window sill a pretty little yellow flower was growing in a crack, bathed in sunshine and rocking in the breeze.

How could gloomy forebodings have arisen amid such sweet sensations? Drenched in air and sunshine, I could think of nothing but freedom; hope beat in my breast as the sun beat down, and I serenely awaited my sentence as one who counts on release and life.

Meanwhile, my counsel arrived. He had been delayed by a hearty breakfast, eaten with good appetite. As he reached his seat, he leaned smilingly over to me. 'There is still hope,' he said.

'I'm sure there is,' I replied, relaxed, and smiling myself.

'Most definitely,' he went on. 'We don't yet know how they have found, but since they can hardly believe you guilty of premeditation, it will be hard labour for life.'

'What are you saying, sir?' I replied indignantly. 'Death is infinitely to be preferred.'

Yes, death! 'And anyway,' some inner voice prompted me, 'I can say so without tempting fate. When have death sentences ever been pronounced except at midnight, by flickering torchlight, in a dingy, black courtroom, on a cold and rainy winter's night? But in August, at eight in the morning, on such a fine day, and with such decent jurors, it would be unthinkable!' And my eyes moved back to the pretty yellow flower in the sunlight.

Just then the president of the court, who had only been waiting for my counsel to appear, bid me stand up. The guard shouldered arms, and at once all the onlookers were on their feet. An unprepossessing individual seated at a table beneath the judges' dais, who must have been the clerk of court, stood to address the assembly and read out the verdict that the jury had pronounced in my absence. My limbs were suddenly drenched in cold sweat, and I leaned against the wall so as not to collapse.

'Counsel for the defence, have you anything to say in mitigation of the sentence?' asked the presiding judge.

It was for me to have plenty to say, but nothing occurred to me. My tongue stayed glued to the roof of my mouth.

My defence counsel stood up.

I saw that he was trying to soften the jury's verdict and to substitute, for the sentence that it carried, the lesser one that I had been so outraged to find him anticipating.

My indignation must have been strong indeed to have surfaced amid this multitude of emotions conflicting in me. I tried to shout out loud what I had already told him, 'Death is infinitely to be preferred!' But words failed me, and I could do no more than grab him roughly by the arm, crying desperately, 'No!'

The king's attorney refuted my counsel, and I listened to him in dumb satisfaction. Then the judges retired, returned, and the president read out my sentence.

'Condemned to death!' howled the crowd; and as I was being led away the entire room rushed after me with the roar of a building collapsing, while I walked on as if drunk and drugged. I had suffered a sea change. Before hearing my death sentence I was aware that my lungs breathed, that my heart beat, and that my body lived in the community of other men; now I plainly saw that a barrier had sprung up between them and me. Nothing was the same as before. The windows brimming with light, the beautiful sun, the clear blue sky, the pretty flower, all of these had turned deathly pale, the colour of a shroud. These men, women, and children who crowded behind me all looked like ghosts.

At the foot of the stairs, a dirty, black vehicle with barred windows awaited me. As I was climbing in, I gazed idly around the square. 'He's condemned to death!' shouted the bystanders as they ran towards the carriage. Through the mist which seemed to have settled between the outside world and me, I made out two young women who were gazing in rapt attention. 'It'll be six weeks from now,' said the younger, clapping her hands.

3

Condemned to death!

Well, why not? *Men*, as I remember reading in some book or other, *are all condemned to death, though the stay of execution varies*. So how has my condition changed?

Since the time when my sentence was pronounced, think how many have died who were all set for a long life! How many young, free, and healthy beings departed this life prematurely, when they were fully expecting to see me beheaded one day on the Place de Grève! And before that day dawns, how many are there now living, breathing, and going about their affairs in total freedom, who will yet die before me!

Anyway, what part of my life will I truly miss? For the gloom and the black bread of my confinement, the ration of vegetable broth drawn from the convicts' bucket, the rough treatment that is so offensive to an educated man, the casual brutality of gaolers and guards, the lack of a living soul who would deign to speak to me and to whom I might reply, the continual trembling for what I have done and for what will be done to me, all these are perhaps the only privileges that the executioner can take away from me.

Yet for all that, it is just appalling!

4

The black carriage transported me to this loathsome place, Bicêtre.

When seen from some distance off, the building looks quite imposing. Set on the brow of a hill, it stretches away into the distance, and from afar retains something of its former splendour, and the appearance of a royal residence. But as you draw nearer, the palace turns into a hovel. The dilapidated eaves are an eyesore. There is something shameful and poverty-stricken that detracts from this royal façade: it's as though the walls are diseased. No single pane of glass remains in any window, naught but heavy, criss-crossed iron bars against which here and there is pressed the pallid face of a convict or a madman.

Not unlike life, when viewed from close quarters.

5

Hardly had I arrived than strong custodians took me in charge. Every possible precaution was taken: no knife and no fork for my meals; the *straitjacket*, a sort of sailcloth bag, pinioned my arms; their job was to keep me alive. My appeal was under way, a cumbersome procedure that could drag on for six or seven weeks, and I was to be delivered in prime condition to the Place de Grève.

For the first few days, I was treated with kindness that was repugnant to me. A warder's respect reeks of the scaffold. Thankfully, habit took over after a few days, when they treated me with the same brutality as the rest of the prisoners, and no longer with the degree of extra politeness that always put me in mind of the executioner. This was not the only improvement. My youth, my submissive behaviour, the prison chaplain's intercession, and in particular a few words of Latin that I spoke to the uncomprehending head gaoler, earned me the privilege of walking once a week with the other prisoners and having the constricting straitjacket removed. After initial reluctance, they also provided me with ink, paper, pens and a night-light.

Every Sunday, after mass, I am allowed into the yard at exercise time. There I chat with the prisoners; it's hard not to. The poor devils are good sorts. They talk about their little *scams*, deeds that would make your hair stand on end if you thought that they were true. They teach me to talk in their slang, *the old clatter and clang*, as they call it. It's a whole new language grafted onto everyday parlance like a loathsome swelling or a wart. Sometimes it has a force that is particularly striking and horrifyingly vivid, as in *there's plonk in a puddle* (blood on the road), or *getting hitched to the widow* (being hanged), with the gallows rope supposed to be the survivor of its previous victims. A thief's head has two names: the *dreaming spire*, when with reasoned premeditation it embarks on crime; *yer nut*, when the executioner cuts it off. Sometimes there are music-hall gags, like a *wicker shawl* for a ragman's basket, or the *tell-tale tit* for the tongue; and constantly recurring are weird, arcane, ugly and sordid words of unknown origin: *blade runner* (the headsman), *the bucket* (death), *treading the boards* (at the scene of the execution). They sound like toads and spiders. When you hear this language spoken, it's like a bundle of filthy, scabby rags being shaken in your face.

At least those men feel sorry for me, but they are the only ones. I know it can't be helped, but the gaolers, warders, and turnkeys laugh, joke, and speak of me in my presence as though I were an object.

6

I thought to myself:

Since I have the means to write, why don't I? But write what? I am trapped between four walls of bare, cold stone, my very steps are circumscribed, and I have nothing to fix my eyes on. My sole pastime during the day is to follow the slow progress of the white square cast by the judas window of my door on the dark wall opposite, and I am, as I said at the beginning, alone with but a single thought, of crime and punishment, killing and death! What can there be for me to say, a man who has nothing more to do in this world? And what shall I find in this despised and vacant brain that is even worth writing down?

And yet, why shouldn't I? Though everything about me is drab and predictable, do not storm, strife, and tragedy rage within me? Does not the obsessional idea which possesses me appear every hour and every minute in new guise, ever more bloody and horrifying as the end draws nigh? Why should I not simply relate to myself the violent and strange sensations I experience in my forsaken condition? It is a rich vein and, short though my life may be, there will be sufficient in the anguish, the terror, and the torture that fill it from now until the final hour to wear out this pen and drain this well dry of ink. And since the only way to alleviate these mental torments is to study them, perhaps writing about them will ease my mind.

Besides, what I write may not be irrelevant. If I have the strength to continue this diary of my sufferings hour by hour, minute by minute, torment by torment, until the moment of its *physical* curtailment, will such a record of my feelings, of necessity unfinished but as detailed as possible, not be a great and inspiring lesson? In this transcript of the last spasms of a dying mind, in this calibrated, upward progression of pain, in this near dissection of a condemned man's intellect, surely there will be food for thought for those who sit in judgement? Will reading it perhaps make them less prompt on some future occasion to throw a head that thinks, the head of a man, onto what they call the scales of justice? What if these uncaring men have never duly considered the slow gradation of tortures summed up in the curt formulation of a death sentence? Have they ever dwelt on the harrowing thought that in the man they eliminate there is an intelligence, one that was entitled to live, and a soul unprepared for death? No, their eyes are riveted on the vertical fall of a triangular blade, and no doubt they think that for the man condemned there is nothing before it, nor anything after.

These pages will cause them to think again. If one day they are published, people must needs pause to reflect on the mental suffering involved; for it is precisely this that they are unaware of. They are smugly proud that they can kill almost painlessly. Heavens, as if that were the question! What is physical pain beside its moral counterpart? O horror and pity, can such laws really exist? A day will surely come, brought closer, I hope by these memoirs, the final disclosures of an unfortunate victim, when...

But who is to say that after my death the wind shall not whip these papers across the muddy prison yard, or plaster them over the cracks in some gaoler's window, where slowly they will rot in the rain?

7

If what I write here can one day be useful to others, causing the judge to pause in mid-sentence and saving other poor devils, whether innocent or guilty, from the death agony to which I am condemned... But so what? why bother? what's the use? When my head has been cut off, what difference does it make to me if they cut off others? Did I really have such delusions? Of demolishing the scaffold after I had climbed it myself? A fat lot of good that would do me, I'm sure.

What! shall the sun, spring, fields of flowers, birds awakening in the morning, clouds, trees, nature, liberty, life, shall all of these things be mine no longer?

No! they can start by saving me! Can it be true that there's no hope, that I must die tomorrow, maybe today, that so it is ordained? Oh, God! the thought is so torturing that you could do the job for them against your own cell wall!

8

Let me calculate what I have left:

Three days' grace after sentence is passed, to decide whether or not to appeal.

A week's delay in the clerk of court's office, after which the *papers*, as they call them, are sent to the Ministry.

Two weeks spent lying at the Ministry, where nobody has the faintest idea that they exist, although they are supposed to be forwarded, after due scrutiny, to the Court of Appeal.

There they are filed, numbered, and noted; for the guillotine is busy, and you must wait your turn.

Two weeks to make sure that nobody jumps your place in the queue.

At last, the Court is convened, normally on a Thursday, rejects twenty appeals *en bloc*, and they go back to the Minister, thence to the Attorney-General, thence to the executioner. Three days.

On the morning of the fourth day, the Attorney-General's deputy thinks, while he is knotting his tie, 'We'd better get this one over and done with.' So then, if the clerk of court's assistant does not have a prior lunch engagement, the execution order is drafted, written up, corrected, and sent off, and from dawn the next day carpenters may be heard assembling a wooden structure on the Place de Grève, and street barkers hoarsely drumming up crowds in the public places.

Six weeks in all. The girl was not wrong.

Well, I've been here in this cell in Bicêtre for at least five weeks, maybe six, for I hardly dare count, and I have a sneaking suspicion that three days ago was a Thursday.

9

I have just drawn up my will.

What for? I was found guilty with costs, and all that I have will scarcely be enough. The guillotine is very expensive.

I leave behind a mother, a wife, and a child.

A little girl of three, gentle, rosy-cheeked, and delicate, with big black eyes and long brown hair.

She was two years and one month old when I last saw her.

So my death will leave three women, one with no son, one with no husband, and one with no father; in different respects they are each of them orphans, three widows by law.

I accept that I am justly punished; but what have these innocent creatures done? No matter, they will be dishonoured and ruined. Such is justice.

I do not fear for my poor old mother: she is sixty-four, and it will kill her. Perhaps she may last for a few days longer, uncomplaining as long as she is given a few hot ashes for her footwarmer.

I do not fear for my wife, either: she is already in poor health and weak of mind. She too will die.

Unless she goes mad, for madness is said to prolong life. At least, though, the mind does not suffer, being asleep and as dead.

But the thought of my daughter, my child, my poor little Marie who even now is laughing, playing, and singing in blissful ignorance, is torture to me!

This is what my cell is like.

Eight feet by eight. Four walls of stone blocks set at right angles to a flagged floor that is one step higher than the outer corridor.

To the right of the door, as you enter, is a shallow nook, an apology for an alcove. A bale of straw is thrown down there and the prisoner must manage to rest and sleep on it, dressed summer and winter alike in sailcloth trousers and a twill jacket.

Above my head, and what I call sky, is a dark ceiling in the style that they call a Gothic vault, from which thick spiders' webs hang down like tattered ribbons.

What else? No windows, not even a skylight. A door of wood clad in iron.

Well, not altogether: in the middle of the upper half of the door is an opening nine inches square, bisected by crossed bars, which the gaoler can close at night.

Outside runs quite a long corridor, lit and ventilated by narrow skylights set high on the wall, and divided into brickwork compartments that communicate with one another through a series of low, arched doors; each of these compartments is what you might call the ante-room to a cell such as mine. These cells contain convicts who have been moved there by the prison governor for disciplinary reasons. The first three are reserved for prisoners condemned to death, because they are nearer to the lodge and hence more convenient for the head warder.

These cells are all that remains of the former Château de Bicêtre, as it was built in the fifteenth century by the Cardinal of Winchester, the one who burned Jeanne d'Arc. I heard this story told to some *sightseers*, who were let into the ante-room to see me yesterday and stared at me from a safe distance as if I were some circus animal. I saw the warder being given a five-franc piece.

I forgot to say that night and day there is a man on guard in front of my cell door, so that my glance never strays to the square peep-hole without meeting his two wide, staring eyes.

Lastly, air and light somehow get into this stone compartment.

Since day has not yet broken, what can be done to while away the night? I had an idea. I got up and played my lantern over the four walls of my cell. They are covered with writing, drawings, strange shapes, and names that overlap and cancel one another out. It seems that, here if nowhere else, each condemned prisoner wanted to leave his mark. In pencil, chalk, or charcoal, in letters that are black, white, or grey, often scored deep into the stone; here and there rusty-coloured letters appear to have been written in blood. Why, if only my mind were more at ease, this strange book, whose pages turn before my eyes on each stone of the cell, would fascinate me. I would enjoy patching together these snatches of thought scattered over the stone, resurrecting each man from beneath his name, breathing meaning and life into these amputated signatures, these thoughts torn limb from limb, these words truncated like the headless bodies that wrote them.

Level with my bed-head are two burning hearts with an arrow running through them, and written above: *Till death do us part.* The poor devil did not enter into a lengthy commitment.

Next to it, a sort of tricorn hat, and beneath it a crudely drawn little face and these words: *Long live the Emperor! 1824.*

Beyond that, more flaming hearts and this inscription, typical of a prison: *I love and worship Mathieu Danvin to death.* JACQUES.

On the opposite wall can be read the name Papavoine. The capital P is most lavishly illuminated with arabesque scrolls.

Then two verses from a filthy song.

A Phrygian cap engraved quite deeply in the stone, and underneath: *Bories. The Republic.* He was one of the four sergeants of La Rochelle. Poor young man! And how appalling was their ruthless dedication to a political chimera, when the reward for an idea, a dream or an abstraction is the terrible reality we call the guillotine! Am I not pathetic, having committed a true crime in which blood was spilled, to feel sorry for myself?

I shall look no further: I just saw, chalked on the wall in the corner, a dreadful picture, the shape of the scaffold which at this very moment may be going up for me. The lamp almost fell from my hands.

12

I rushed back to my straw and sank down, putting my head between my knees. Then my childish panic gave way to a morbid desire to continue reading my wall.

From beside Papavoine's name I tore down a huge spider's web, encrusted with dust and stretching right across the corner. Beneath this web were four or five perfectly legible names, amid others that are no more than a smudge on the wall. DAUTUN, 1815. POULAIN, 1818. JEAN MARTIN, 1821. CASTAING, 1823. I read these names, and grim memories came back to me: of Dautun, the man who cut his brother into four pieces and roamed Paris at night, throwing the head into a fountain and the trunk into a sewer; of Poulain, the man who killed his wife; of Jean Martin, the man who shot his father as the old man was opening a window; of Castaing, the doctor who poisoned his friend, and who treated him in the final illness he had brought on by giving him, not an antidote, but more poison; and beside theirs, the name of Papavoine, the gruesome madman who killed children by knifing them in the head![19]

Well, I thought, as a feverish shudder ran through my lower body, so these were the occupants of this cell before me. Here, on this very floor, these bloodthirsty killers thought their last thoughts! Like wild animals, they paced around the tight square enclosed by these walls. They followed one another in quick succession; it is said that the cell rarely lies empty for long. They kept the place warm, and warm for me. And I shall follow in their footsteps to be buried at Clamart, where the grass grows so green!

I am not a dreamer or a superstitious person. No doubt my thoughts had made me slightly feverish, for while I was musing, it suddenly seemed that these fatal names were written in fire on the black wall. My ears were bursting from a ringing din that grew faster and faster; a red veil swam before my eyes; then I felt that the cell was full of men, strange men who were carrying their heads in their left hands, gripping them by the mouth because they had no hair. They all shook their right fists at me, except the man who had killed his father.

I shut my eyes in horror, only to see everything with greater clarity.

Dream, vision, or actual event, I think I would have gone mad if a sudden sensation had not wakened me in time. As I was on the point of falling backwards, I felt a cold belly and hairy legs crawling across my bare foot; the spider I had disturbed was making its escape.

That brought me to my senses. No horrid spectral beings these, but mere vapours, a phantom of my costive and overwrought brain. A Macbethian procession! The dead are good and dead, and none more so than these. They are safely locked up in the grave, which is not a prison from which escape is possible. How then did I come to be so terribly afraid?

The door of the grave cannot be opened from within.

13

A few days ago, I saw a most hideous sight.

It was hardly light, yet the prison was filled with noise. Heavy doors could be heard opening and slamming, bolts and heavy iron padlocks squealing, bunches of keys jingling on the warders' belts, stairs juddering from top to bottom under hurrying feet, and voices shouting to one another from either end of the long corridors. My cell neighbours, convicts in solitary confinement, were in better humour than usual. The whole of Bicêtre seemed to be laughing, singing, running, and dancing.

As the only one remaining silent in this bedlam, and standing still in this stampede, I listened in wide-eyed amazement.

A warder passed by.

I plucked up the courage to call out to him, asking if it was a holiday in the prison.

'You can call it that if you like!' he replied. 'Today they put the irons on the convicts who are off to Toulon tomorrow. If you fancy it, it's well worth seeing.'

Any diversion at all, however disgusting, was welcome to a

solitary detainee. I accepted his offer to look on.

The warder took the usual precautions against my escape, then led me into a small, unoccupied and totally empty cell; this had a barred window, but nevertheless a real one you could lean your elbows on and through which the sky could actually be seen.

'You'll see and hear everything from here,' he said. 'You've got your own private box, just like the King'.

Then he went out, locking, padlocking, and bolting me in.

The window looked out over quite a broad, square courtyard that was walled in on four sides by a tall, six-storey stone building. Nothing could be more sordid, squalid, or offensive to the eye than this four-sided frontage of innumerable barred windows; they were all of them crammed from top to bottom like the bricks in a wall, with a multitude of gaunt, pale faces, these framed, as it were, between the criss-crossed iron bars. These were the prisoners, an audience at present but waiting their turn to be performers. They looked like the souls of the damned peeking into hell through the window-slits of purgatory.

All stared silently at the courtyard, which remained empty. Among those dull and dejected faces a few eyes blazed here and there, keen and lively as sparks.

The prison square which is built around the courtyard is not entirely enclosed. One of the four wings of the building (the one facing east) has an opening in the middle and is joined to the next part only by an iron gate. This gate gives on to a second courtyard, smaller than the first, and similarly overhung by grimy walls and gables.

Right round the main courtyard run stone benches set into the walls. In the middle stands an arched metal post on which a lantern clock can be hung.

The clock struck midday. A big carriage gateway, hidden in a recess of the wall, swung open suddenly, and a wagon, escorted by a dirty, ruffianly crew of soldiers in blue uniforms with red epaulettes and yellow shoulder straps trundled heavily into the yard with a loud metallic din. This was the convict escort bringing the chains.

Just then, as if only this encouragement were needed for noise to break out in the rest of the prison, the men at the window, who till then had been still and silent, burst into shouts of joy, began singing, and howled threats and oaths mingled with howls of laughter most distressing to hear. They looked like devil's masks. Every face was twisted in a grimace, every fist was brandished through the bars, every voice bellowed, every eye was ablaze, and I was appalled to see these ashes glow with so many sparks.

Meanwhile their guards, not to be confused with those who, by their clean clothes and dismayed expressions, could be identified as sightseers come from Paris, went calmly about their business. One of them jumped onto the wagon and threw down to his colleagues the chains, the travelling collars, and the bundles of sailcloth trousers. Then they divided up the work; some went to a corner of the yard, where they laid out the long chains which in their slang go by the name of *strings*; others laid out on the cobbles the *taffeta*, the shirts, and the breeches; meanwhile, under the supervision of their captain, a short and stocky old man, the most experienced of them made a careful inspection of each of the iron neck-collars, testing them out by striking them against the cobbles till sparks flew. All this was punctuated by the jeering cheers of the prisoners, above which could be heard the harsh laughter of the convicts for whom these preparations were intended; they were at the windows of the old prison that looks out over the smaller courtyard.

When everything was ready, a man bearing silver regalia, who was addressed as *Monsieur l'Inspecteur*, gave an order to the *Governor* of the prison; and a moment later, two or three low doorways suddenly and almost simultaneously disgorged into the yard wave upon wave of hideous, howling, and ragged men. These were the convicts.

They entered to renewed whoops of joy from the windows. Some of them, as convict celebrities, were greeted with cheers and applause, which they acknowledged with a kind of becoming modesty. The majority of them had hats of a sort that they had woven themselves from the straw in their cells, always bizarrely shaped so that the wearer would be recognised by it in the towns they passed through. The applause for these men was even greater. One in particular, a young man of seventeen with the face of a girl, received a rapturous ovation. He had come from the cell where he had been in solitary confinement for a week; from his bale of straw he had made a garment that clad him head to foot, and he came cartwheeling into the courtyard with snake-like suppleness. He was a strolling player convicted of theft. There were waves of clapping, and joyful shouts. The convicts clapped back, and this mutual encouragement of branded convicts and convicts-to-be was a dreadful prospect. The presence of society, in the persons of the gaolers and the terrified sightseers, seemed an irrelevance: crime sneered and gestured insolently, and turned this degrading punishment into a family celebration.

As they came in, they were propelled between two lines of warders into the smaller, gated yard, where they were to undergo a medical examination. And there they all made one last attempt to postpone their trip, complaining about poor health, bad eyesight, lameness, or an injured hand. But they were almost invariably found fit to travel to the convict station, whereupon each took on an air of jaunty resignation, soon forgetting this lifelong infirmity of his.

The gate of the small courtyard opened once more. A guard called the roll in alphabetical order; they came out one by one, and each convict went and stood in a corner of the main courtyard, next to a companion who was close to him alphabetically. Hence each man is abandoned to himself; each bears his chain by himself, side by side with a stranger; and were the convict to have a friend, the chain-gang separated them. Could human misery be greater?

When thirty or so had emerged, the gate was shut once more. A guard lined them up with his stick, threw down in front of each man a shirt, a jacket, and coarse cloth trousers, then at a given signal they all began to undress. As if on cue, an unexpected occurrence turned this humiliation into torture.

Up to then it had been a reasonably fine day, and if the cold October wind gave a distinct nip to the air, it also opened up gaps in the banks of grey cloud through which a shaft of sunlight could fall. But scarcely had the convicts taken off their prison rags, and just as they were standing naked and being painstakingly frisked by the guards, under the inquisitive gaze of the visitors who were walking round them and looking at their shoulders, the sky blackened and a cold autumnal shower fell suddenly, lashing down torrentially on the square courtyard, on the bare hands and naked limbs of the convicts, and on their miserable clothing spread out on the ground.

In an instant, the yard was emptied of all who were not warders or convicts. The Parisian onlookers took shelter beneath the arches of the gateways.

Meanwhile, the rain was bucketing down. No one could be seen in the yard but the drenched and naked convicts on the streaming cobbles. Their noisy bravado had given way to grim-lipped silence. They were shivering and their teeth were chattering; their skinny legs and bony knees were banging together; and it was heart-rending to watch them trying to protect limbs that were blue with cold with sodden shirts and jackets, and trousers that were dripping wet. Nakedness would have been preferable.

Only one old fellow remained cheerful. He shouted out, as he tried to dry himself with his wet shirt, that *this was not on the agenda*; then he started to laugh, and shook his fist at the sky.

When they had put on their travelling clothes, they were led in groups of twenty or thirty to the other end of the yard, where the ropes laid out on the ground were waiting. These ropes are long and sturdy chains, with shorter chains crossing at right angles every two feet; at either end of these is fixed a square collar, which opens by means of a hinge in one corner and is closed in the opposite corner by an iron rivet, and it stays bolted round the convict's neck while he is in transit. When these ropes are laid on the ground, they look not unlike the bones of a fish.

The convicts were made to sit down in the mud on the flooded cobblestones; their collars were tried; then two smiths from their escort, bearing portable anvils, cold-riveted them on with mighty sledgehammer blows. A dreadful moment, and one that makes the bravest quail. Each hammer-blow struck on the anvil leaning against his back makes the victim's chin jerk upwards; the least lateral movement, and his skull would be cracked open like a nut.

After this had been done, they fell sullenly silent. Nothing was heard but the jingling of the chains, and from time to time a howl and the thud of the guards' truncheons on the limbs of a recalcitrant. Some there were who wept; the old men shivered and bit their lips. I gazed in terror on all these sinister silhouettes in their iron frames.

Thus, after the doctors' inspection comes the warders' inspection; and after the warders' inspection, the chaining. Three acts to the play.

A ray of sunlight broke through. It seemed to fire their brains. The convicts all got up at once, as if jerked by a spasm. The five chain-gangs suddenly joined hands and formed a giant circle around the lantern post. They revolved till you grew giddy. They were singing a convict song, a slang ballad, in a tune that at times was plaintive, and at times harshly jocular; now and then shrill cries and panting screeches of laughter could be heard mingling with the arcane words; then thunderous applause; and the clashing chains that beat time were an orchestral accompaniment to this choir, whose hoarse songs drowned it out. If ever I sought to depict a witches' sabbath, I could not do better or worse than this.

A large cooking-pot was carried into the yard. The guards swung their clubs and broke up the convicts' dance, then led them over to the pot, in which some vegetables or other were floating in a steaming, dirty liquid. They ate.

And when they had eaten, they cast onto the cobbles what remained of their soup and their coarse bread, and started once more to dance and to sing. It is customary to grant them this privilege on the day they are chained and the night that follows.

I watched this singular spectacle with such rapt, involved, and absorbed attention that I had forgotten myself entirely. I was shaken to the core with pity, and their laughter made me cry.

Suddenly, through the haze of the daydream into which I had fallen, I saw the shrieking reel stop and fall silent. Then all eyes turned towards my window. 'Death Row! Death Row!' they shouted, all pointing to me; and their bursts of merriment grew louder.

I stood petrified.

I do not know in what connection they had heard of me, or how they recognised me.

'Hallo! Goodbye!' was their blackly humorous taunt. The leaden face of one of the youngest, who had been sentenced to hard labour for life, beamed enviously at me, and he said, 'Lucky blighter, he'll be *topped!* So long, pal!'

I cannot describe what I felt just then. For I suppose I *was* their pal. La Grève is twinned with Toulon. I was sunk even lower than they, and they duly acknowledged it. I shuddered.

Yes, I was their pal all right! And a few days later it would have been my turn to put on a show for them.

I had stayed stock-still at the window, stiff and paralysed. But when I saw the five chain-gangs move, then crowd towards me with words of hellish fraternity, and when I heard the deafening noise of their irons, their shouts, and their footsteps down below outside, I thought that this swarm of demons was climbing up to my squalid cell. I screamed and threw myself against the door with a violence fit to break it down, but escape was impossible: it was bolted from the outside. I knocked and cried out frantically. Then I felt that the bloodcurdling convict voices were drawing nearer still. Convinced I could see their horrid heads rising above the sill of my window, I screamed out once more in terror and swooned clean away.

14

When I came to, it was night. I was lying on a pallet bed; by the light of a lantern that hung gently swaying I could see other beds in a row on both sides of mine. I realised that I had been taken to the infirmary.

For a few moments I lay awake, my mind and my memory both blank, beside myself with joy at being in a bed. At one time, of course, this bed in a prison infirmary would have made me blench with disgust and pity; but now I was a different man. The sheets were grey and coarse to the touch, the blanket flimsy and full of holes, and the straw could be felt through the mattress. But what did it matter when my limbs could stretch out and relax under the rough sheets, when beneath the blanket, thin as it was, the persistent chill that numbed me to the bone was at last beginning to thaw? I went back to sleep.

I was woken by a loud noise; it was just after daybreak. The noise came from outside; my bed was next to the window, and I sat up to see what it was.

The window looked out over the main courtyard of Bicêtre. It was so crowded that two lines of veterans were having trouble in clearing a narrow passage across. Between the twin lines of soldiers rolled five long wagons full of men, jolting heavily over every cobblestone. It was the convicts' departure.

These wagons were open, and each chain-gang sat in one of them. The convicts sat straddling each side, the two lines back to back, separated by the communal chain that ran down the middle, and on each end of which stood a guard bearing a loaded rifle. You could hear the clinking of their irons, and at each jolt of the vehicle see their heads jump and their dangling legs swing.

A persistent, fine drizzle chilled the air, plastering against their knees cloth trousers that had turned from grey to black. Their long beards and cropped hair were drenched; their faces were purple; they were visibly shivering and grinding their teeth with rage and with cold. Other than that, no movement was possible. Once you are bolted to this chain, you are no more than a fraction of the hideous entity called the chain-gang, that moves as one man. Your intelligence must surrender, condemned to death by the collar of the convict station; as for the animal part of you, it can have needs and appetites only at given times. Like this, then, sitting still and mostly half-naked, with their heads bare and their legs dangling, they were beginning their twenty-five day journey, transported in the same wagons and wearing the same clothes whether the baking sun of July or the chill rain of November beat down. It is tempting to believe that men enlist the climate as an instrument of torture.

Between the crowds and the wagon passengers a grisly conversation of sorts had been initiated, with insults coming from one side, boasts from the other, and curses from both; but the captain gave a signal and I saw clubs striking down at random of the shoulders and heads in the wagons, whereupon the apparent calm that is called *order* reigned once more. But the eyes of these men blazed vengeance, and the fists of these wretches lay tightly clenched upon their knees.

The five wagons, escorted by gendarmes on horseback and guards on foot, disappeared one by one from view beneath the main carriage exit from Bicêtre; a sixth followed on behind, in which stew pots, pans, and spare chains were rattling from side to side. Some convict guards who had lingered in the canteen came running out to rejoin the escort. The crowd dispersed. The whole sight faded away like a bad dream. Still borne over the air, but gradually dying away, came the sound of the rumbling wheels and the horses' hooves on the cobbled road to Fontainebleau, the crack of the whips, the clinking of the chains, and the jeering of bystanders who sent the convicts packing with a curse.

Yet for them that is only the beginning!

What was it my defence counsel said to me? The galleys! No, death is infinitely to be preferred to this, the scaffold to the convict station, and oblivion to such hell on earth! And Guillotin's blade will kiss my neck more lovingly than the convict collar! Oh, my God, the galleys!

15

But unfortunately there was nothing wrong with me. Next day I had to leave the infirmary. The cell received me back.

Nothing wrong with me? Well, of course, I am young, healthy, and strong. Blood flows freely through my veins; my limbs respond to my every bidding; I am sound in body and mind, and equipped for a long and healthy life. All this is true; and yet I have an illness, a terminal condition, and a man-made one at that.

Since I left the infirmary, a most tormenting and maddening idea came to me, that I might well have escaped if I had been left there.

The doctors and sisters of charity seemed to take an interest in me. I was to die so young, and such a death! They swarmed round my bedside, as though they were sorry for me. But no! just idle curiosity! Anyway, these healers may cure you of a fever, but not of a death sentence. Yet it would be so easy for them! A door could be left open! Why should they mind?

But now my chance has gone for good! My appeal will be turned down, because the trial was properly conducted; the witnesses duly testified, prosecution and defence duly spoke, the judges duly passed judgement. So there is no hope unless… No, this is madness! there is no hope! To appeal is to be suspended by a rope above a sheer drop, and to hear it fraying minute by minute until it breaks. As though the guillotine blade took six weeks to fall.

If I were pardoned? Pardoned! but by whom? on what grounds? and how? There is no way that I could be pardoned. Let us make an example of him! as they say.

There are but three more steps for me to take: Bicêtre, the Conciergerie, La Grève.

16

During the few hours I spent in the prison infirmary, I had been sitting next to a window, enjoying the sun – which had reappeared – or at least as much of the sun as the bars of the window let through.

I sat there with my burning head hanging heavy in my hands, with my elbows on my knees and my feet on the crossbars of my chair; for dejection makes me bend and curl up on myself as though my limbs had no bones, and my flesh no muscles.

The stale prison smell distressed me more than ever, my ears were still ringing from all the noise of convicts and their chains, and I felt sick and tired of Bicêtre. I thought that God should take pity on me, and ought at least to send a little bird to perch on the edge of the roof opposite and sing to me.

I don't know if it was God or the devil who answered my prayer, but just then I heard a voice rising from beneath my window, and not a bird's, but far sweeter: the pure, soft, and innocent voice of a girl of fifteen. My head jerked upright and I listened with rapture to the song that she was singing. It was a slow and soothing melody, and she seemed sadly and mournfully to warble it; the words went as follows:

As I was walking down the alley,
Too-ra-lie, too-ra-lie;
They nabbed me and it weren't too pally,
Too-ra-lay, too-ra-lay,
Three dirty rozzers fell on me,
Too-ra-loo-ra-loo-ra-lie;
They locked me up and lost the key,
Too-ra-lie, too-ra-lie, too-ra-lay.

Words would find it hard to convey the keenness of my disappointment. The voice continued:

They snapped the cuffs around me wrists,
Too-ra-lie, too-ra-lie;
I 'ad no chance, 'cos I was pissed,
Too-ra-lay, too-ra-lay;
The sarge was laughing fit to bust,
Too-ra-loo-ra-loo-ra-lie;
To see me arse dragged through the dust,
Too-ra-loo-ra-loo-ra-lay;
Just then me mucker came in sight,
Too-ra-lie, too-ra-lie, too-ra-lay.

I shouted, 'Mate, this ain't no laugh,
Too-ra-lie, too-ra-lie;
Nip off and tell me better 'alf,
Too-ra-lay, too-ra-lay;
That I've been banged up good and tight.'
Too-ra-loo-ra-loo-ra-lie;
By 'eck, but she was mad all right,
Too-ra-loo-ra-loo-ra-lay;

Sez she, 'Gawd, what yer bin and done?'
Too-ra-lie, too-ra-lie, too-ra-lay.

'Let's 'ear the truth and cut the crap.'
Too-ra-lie, too-ra-lie;
'I chivved a bloke and took the rap,
Too-ra-lay, too-ra-lay;
Off wiv 'is dosh I tried to make,
Too-ra-loo-ra-loo-a-lie;
'Twas worth it for the ticker's sake,
Too-ra-loo-ra-loo-ra-lay;
And buckles worth a bob or two.'
Too-ra-lie, too-ra-lie, too-ra-lay.

The old girl didn't bat an eye,
Too-ra-lie, too-ra-lie;
Cadges a lift down to Versailles,
Too-ra-lay, too-ra-lay;
She burst right in upon the King,
Too-ra-loo-ra-loo-ra-lie;
Promised the bugger anything,
Too-ra-loo-ra-loo-ra-lay;
To spring me from this slammer 'ere,
Too-ra-lie, too-ra-lie, too-ra-lay.

If I get out, I'll tell you this,
Too-ra-lie, too-ra-lie;
She'll get a great big smacking kiss,
Too-ra-lay, too-ra-lay;
I'll buy 'er clothes to wear, all right,
Too-ra-loo-ra-loo-ra-lie;
The family jewels are 'ers that night,
Too-ra-loo-ra-loo-ra-lay;
And pearly clogs will grace 'er feet,
Too-ra-lie, too-ra-lie, too-ra-lay.

But then she laid it on too thick,
Too-ra-lie, too-ra-lie;
And got upon the Guv'nor's wick,
Too-ra-lay, too-ra-lay;
Sez he, 'Just give that tongue a rest,
Too-ra-loo-ra-loo-ra-lie;
Yer old man's future don't look fair,
Too-ra-loo-ra-loo-ra-lay;
I've sentenced 'im to walk on air.'
Too-ra-lie, too-ra-lie, too-ra-lay.

I listened no more, nor could I have done. The half-grasped and half-hidden meaning of this loathsome lament, the struggle between the felon and the constabulary, the thief whom he meets and sends to his wife the dreadful message: I have killed a man and been arrested, *I chivved a bloke and took the rap*; the woman rushing to Versailles with a petition, with this *Guv'nor* who loses his temper and threatens to make the culprit *walk on air*; and all of this sung to the sweetest tune, by the sweetest voice that ever lulled a body to sleep!… I was mortified, chilled and crushed. What a hideous nightmare to hear these foul words springing from such pure and rosy lips. It was like the slime left by a slug on a rose.

I can hardly express what I felt: pain, yet inflicted with such loving strokes. To hear the patois of the robbers' lair and the hulks, a vile, slangy jargon both bloody and grotesque, borne on the voice of a girl that is on that fine cusp between a child's and a woman's! And for all these misshapen and deformed words to be sung, phrased and trilled!

Oh, what a hateful place a prison is! Its poison corrupts everything. Nothing survives its withering blast, not even the song of a girl of fifteen! You may find a bird there, but it has mud on its wing; and if you pick a pretty flower to breathe its fragrance, why, it stinks.

17

Oh! if I escaped, how I would run through the fields!

No sense in running, though. That draws attention to you and awakens suspicion. Walk slowly instead, with head held high, and sing. Try to get hold of an old blue smock embroidered in red. It's a good disguise. The gardeners round here all wear them.

Near Arcueil, I know where there is a clump of trees by marshy ground; I used to go there every Thursday with my school friends to catch frogs. I could hide in it until evening.

After nightfall, I would continue my journey. I would go to Vincennes. No: I couldn't cross the river. I would go to Arpajon. But I would have done better to go off in the Saint-Germain direction, head for Le Havre, and from there catch a boat to England. Well, anyway, I get as far as Longjumeau. Then a gendarme goes by, and asks to see my passport… The game is up!

You fond dreamer, begin by demolishing the stone wall three feet thick that imprisons you! O death! death!

And to think that I used to come to Bicêtre as a child, so that I could look down the great wall and see the madmen!

18

While I was writing all this, my lamp grew dimmer, day broke, and the chapel clock struck six.

But what does this mean? The duty warder just came into my cell, doffed his cap respectfully, apologised for disturbing me and asked gently as his rough voice permits what I would like for breakfast…

I shivered suddenly. Does that mean it's for today?

Yes, it's for today!

The prison governor himself has just paid me a visit. He asked me if there was any way he could oblige me or be of service, said that he hoped I had no complaint against him or any of his staff, enquired courteously about my health and the way I had slept, and on his way out he called me *sir*!

It's for today, all right!

This gaoler does not believe that I have grounds for complaint against him or his minions. And he is right. It would be churlish of me to complain: they have done their job, and guarded me well, were courteous when I arrived and when I left. I have no cause for dissatisfaction, now have I?

This good gaoler, with his indulgent smile, his soft words, his obsequious but inquisitive eyes, and his big, broad hands, is the prison made flesh, Bicêtre made man. Everything around me is a prison; I find the prison in every shape and form, in human guise as much as in the bars or in the bolts. This wall is a prison of stone; this door is a prison of wood; these warders are a prison of flesh and blood. Prison is some loathsome creature, one and indivisible, half building and half man. I am its prey; it fondles me and clasps me to its bosom. It shuts me within its granite walls, behind its lock and its key, and watches over me with its guard's eyes.

Poor devil that I am! what will become of me? and what will they do to me?

21

I am calm now. It is over, quite, quite over. I am rid of the dreadful fright the governor's visit put me into. For I have to admit that I had not lost hope. But now, thank God, there is none left.

This is what just happened.

Just as half-past six – no, a quarter to seven – was striking, the door of my cell opened again. A white-haired old man wearing a brown frock coat came in. He began to undo it. I saw a cassock and clerical bands. It was a priest.

This priest was not the prison chaplain, and that did not augur well.

Smiling indulgently, he sat down opposite me; then he nodded his head and looked heavenwards, or at least at the ceiling of the cell. I understood his meaning.

'My son,' he said to me, 'are you prepared?'

I replied faintly, 'I am not prepared, yet I am ready.'

But as I said this, everything swam before my eyes, icy sweat gushed from every part of my body, I felt my temples throb, and my ears were filled with a buzzing noise.

While I swayed on my chair as if asleep, the kindly old man spoke. Or so I believe, for I think I saw his lips moving, his hands waving, and his eyes shining.

The door now opened a second time. The squeal of bolts being drawn wrenched me from my stupor and him from his speech. A gentleman of sorts, dressed in black and accompanied by the prison governor, introduced himself with a deep bow. The man's expression bore signs of that occupational solemnity common in undertakers. In his hand he carried a rolled-up paper.

'Sir,' he said with an ingratiating smile, 'I am *huissier* to the Royal Court of Paris. I have the honour to bring you a communication from the Attorney-General.'

The first shock had passed. My presence of mind returned to me.

'You mean,' I replied, 'the Attorney-General who was so insistent in demanding my head? The honour is mine, I'm sure, if he deigns to write to me. I hope that he will be pleased when I die, for I would hate to think that he grew so warm in pursuit of a head that meant little to him.'

Having said all this, I continued calmly, 'Read it to me, sir.'

He began to read out a long document, stumbling over every other word and with his voice rising at the end of each line. My appeal was rejected.

'Sentence will be carried out today on the Place de Grève,' he concluded, without looking up from his piece of stamped paper. 'We shall leave for the Conciergerie at half past seven precisely. My dear sir, will you please be ready to accompany me?'

For the last few moments I had not been listening to him. The governor was talking to the priest, and this man was still staring at his paper. I looked towards the door, which lay open … What madness! There were four soldiers with rifles in the corridor!

The *huissier* repeated his question, looking at me this time.

'Whenever you like,' I replied. 'At your good pleasure.'

He bowed to me, saying, 'I shall have the honour of calling for you in half an hour.'

Then they left me alone.

Oh, God! I have got to get out! In any way at all! I must escape, I must! Right now! Through doors, through windows, or through the roof! and even if I leave pieces of my flesh clinging to the beams!

But, curses! hell and damnation! it would take months to tunnel through this wall with good tools, and I don't have even a nail, or even an hour!

22

From the Conciergerie

Well, I have been *transferred*, as the official jargon puts it.

But the journey is well worth describing.

As it was striking half past seven, the *huissier* stood once more at the doorway of my cell. 'Sir,' he said, 'I am ready for you.' Alas! he is not the only one.

I got up and took one step; but I thought that a second was beyond my power, my head felt so heavy and my legs so weak. Yet I took hold of myself, and went on walking fairly steadily. Before leaving the cell I looked round it one last time, for I loved my cell. Then I left it empty and open, which is a strange way for a cell to look.

Anyway, it will not be like that for long. Someone is expected this evening, said the turnkey, a man on whom the assize court is even now passing sentence.

At the point where the corridor branched off, we were met by the chaplain. He had just eaten breakfast.

As I was leaving the prison building, the governor shook my hand warmly, and added four veteran soldiers to my escort.

A dying old man who had been laid out at the door of the infirmary cried out, 'See you soon!'

We arrived in the courtyard. I took deep breaths, and this revived me.

We did not walk for long in the open air. A carriage drawn by post-horses was standing in the outer courtyard; it was the one that had brought me, a sort of rectangular cabriolet divided widthways into two sections by a grille of mesh so stout that it seems knitted. Both compartments have a door, one at the front and one at the back of the carriage. And the whole contraption is so dirty, black, and dusty that in comparison, a pauper's hearse is like a coronation carriage.

Before burying myself in this two-wheeled grave, I gazed round the courtyard with a look so despairing that it could have brought the walls down. This yard, like a little square planted with trees, was more crowded with onlookers than it had been for the convicts. Crowds already!

As on the day that the chain-gang had left, a seasonal icy drizzle was falling; it still is at the time of writing, and will probably fall all day, outlasting me.

The roadways were potholed, and the whole yard swimming in slime and water. I was pleased to see the crowd knee-deep in such mud.

We got in, the *huissier* and a gendarme going into the forward compartment, and the priest, myself, and a gendarme in the other. Four mounted gendarmes around the carriage. Eight men against one, not counting the coachman.

As I climbed in, an old woman with grey eyes was saying, 'Why, this is better than the chain-gang.'

That I can understand. It is a sight that is taken in more easily and quickly at a glance. It is equally striking, and more convenient. There are no distractions: just one man, but weighed down by as much misfortune as all the convicts put together. Yet it is less diffuse, a concentrated and more aromatic liqueur.

The carriage jerked into motion. With a dull rumble it sped out through the main gate into the avenue, and the heavy double doors of Bicêtre swung to behind it. I was driven off in a state of stupefaction, like a man in a cataleptic state who can neither move nor cry out, but knows he is being buried. I could just about hear the bells round the post-horses' necks jingling in rhythmical, coughing bursts, the iron-shod wheels clattering over the cobbles or battering against the coachwork as they jolted from rut to rut, the thundering gallop of the mounted escort, and the crack of the coachman's whip. It all seemed like a whirlwind that was whisking me away.

Through a barred peep-hole across from me, my eyes had come mechanically to rest on the inscription carved in huge letters above the main gate of Bicêtre: OLD PEOPLE'S HOME.

'Well, well,' I thought, 'so people spend their retirement here.'

And, just as we do in the time between waking and sleeping, I turned this thought over and over in my pain-befuddled mind. Suddenly the carriage turned from the avenue onto the main highway, and the vision through the peep-hole changed. The towers of Notre-Dame were now framed in it, blue and half-hidden in the haze of Paris. So now the image in my mind changed too: I had become as mechanical as the vehicle. The thought of Bicêtre was supplanted by the thought of the towers of Notre-Dame. 'The ones standing on the tower by the flag-pole will have a good view,' I thought to myself, smiling fatuously.

I think it was then the priest began to speak to me once more. My ears were already ringing with the noise of the wheels, the galloping hooves, and the coachman's whip. It was just one more noise.

I listened in silence to his monotonous cascade of words, that lulled me into drowsiness like the gentle plashing of a fountain, going by me never the same and yet never different, like the gnarled elms along the highway, when the curt, clipped voice of the *huissier* sitting up front suddenly jolted me awake. 'Well, Father,' he asked almost cheerily, 'let's hear the latest news.'

He turned his body towards the priest as he said this.

The chaplain had not stopped talking to me and, deafened by the din of the carriage, did not reply.

'I say, there!' the *huissier* continued, raising his voice to compete with the noise of the wheels. 'Damn this carriage!'

Damn it indeed!

He went on, 'This road noise certainly kills the art of conversation. What was I trying to say, now? Did you catch what I was trying to say there, Father? Oh, yes, what's the main story from Paris today?'

I shuddered, as though he were speaking about me.

'Sorry,' said the priest, when at last he heard him, 'I have not had time to read the papers this morning. I won't know until evening. When I am busy all day like this, I tell the gateman to keep the papers for me, and read them when I get back.'

'Come on,' the *huissier* interrupted. 'You must have heard, one way or another. The story of the day from Paris! The morning's main story!'

I spoke up, saying, 'I think I know what it is.'

The *huissier* looked at me. 'You! how can you know? Well, then, what is it?'

'You seem eager to be informed,' I said to him.

'Why not, sir?' the *huissier* retorted. 'Every man is entitled to his political views, and I would be doing you an injustice if I thought that you did not have yours. Well, *I* am all for the National Guard being reconstituted[10]. I was the sergeant of my company and we had some rare good times, I can tell you.'

I interrupted him, saying, 'No, I don't think it had anything to do with that.'

'So what was it, if you claim to know the day's news?'

'I was referring to another major talking-point in Paris today.'

The fool did not understand; his curiosity was whetted.

'Some other news? And where the devil would you get hold of it? I'm sorry, please tell me what it is, my dear sir. Do you know what it is, Father? Are you better informed than I am? Put me in the picture, I beg you. What is it? I can't help it, I just love to hear the news. I pass it on to the president of the court, and he likes that.'

There was much more of this nonsense. He looked in turn at the priest and then me, and my only reply was to shrug my shoulders.

'Come on', he said, 'what was it you had in mind?'

'What I had in mind,' I replied, 'is that this evening I shall have nothing in mind.'

'Oh! is that all?' he replied. 'Heavens, why be so gloomy? Doctor Castaing was quite chatty.' After a moment's silence, he went on, 'I accompanied Monsieur Papavoine; he was wearing his otterskin cap and smoking a cigar. But the young men of La Rochelle talked only to one another. Still, they did talk.' He paused once more, then continued, 'Madmen! Fanatics! They seemed to despise everybody. But your problem, young man, is that you are a good deal too withdrawn.'

'Young man, am I?' I said to him. 'I am older than you are; each quarter of an hour that goes by adds a year to my life.'

He turned around, gazed on me for a few minutes as he struggled to understand, then began to snigger knowingly. 'You're having me on! Older than me? I could be your grandfather.'

'I'm not joking,' I replied solemnly.

He opened his snuffbox. 'My dear sir, pray don't be offended; here, take a pinch, and try not to think badly of me.'

'Don't worry, it wouldn't be for long.'

At that moment, the snuffbox he was holding out to me touched the wire grille that separated us. A particularly deep rut jolted them against one another, and it fell, spilling its contents under the gendarme's feet.

'Blast that grille!' shouted the *huissier*. He turned towards me. 'What rotten luck, eh? I've lost all my snuff.'

'I stand to lose more than you,' I replied with a smile.

He tried to gather up the snuff again, mumbling to himself, 'Lose more than me! that's easy to say. All the way to Paris with no snuff! Is that not terrible?'

The chaplain then uttered some words of consolation, and perhaps my mind was elsewhere, but I had the impression that it was the second part of the sermon of which I had had the beginning. Gradually the priest and the *huissier* struck up a conversation; I let them talk, and for my part began to think.

Perhaps my mind was still elsewhere when we arrived at the city limits, but Paris seemed noisier to me than usual.

The carriage stopped for a moment at the tollbooth. The city tax officials inspected it. If it had been a sheep or an ox being led to the slaughter they would have required their tribute of silver; but no dues are payable on a human head. We passed through.

Once the boulevard had been crossed, the carriage drove briskly into the old, winding streets of the Saint-Marceau district and the Cité, which twist and bisect one another like the thousands of galleries in an anthill. The carriage gained pace over the cobbles of these narrow streets, clattering so loudly that I could hear none of the noises outside. When I glanced through the little square window, I thought that the streams of passers-by were stopping to look at the carriage, and gangs of children running in its wake. It seemed to me also that here and there in the public places an old man or woman in rags, and occasionally both, their mouths frozen in mid-cry, could be seen holding aloft a bunch of printed sheets that people fought over.

The clock of the Palais de Justice was striking half past eight when we turned into the entrance yard of the Conciergerie. I was chilled by the sight of the great staircase, the black chapel and the gloomy gatehouses. When the carriage stopped, I felt that my heart too would stop beating.

I gathered up my remaining strength; the door flew open with lightning speed, I jumped down from the mobile cell, and sped between two lines of soldiers through the gate. Already a crowd had had time to gather.

23

While I walked in the public galleries of the Palais de Justice I felt almost free and relaxed; but my courage deserted me when I was shown through low doorways, down hidden staircases, inner passageways, and long, stale and muffled-sounding corridors accessible only to those who pass or receive sentence.

The *huissier* was still by my side. The priest had gone off for two hours, having business to attend to.

I was taken to the governor's office, and placed by the *huissier* in his keeping. It was an exchange, because the governor asked him to wait for a moment, adding that he had a client to hand over to him, to be taken without delay to Bicêtre on the return journey of the carriage. No doubt it was the man sentenced today, who will sleep tonight on the bale of straw that I had not sufficient time to wear out.

'Fine,' the *huissier* said to the governor, 'then I'll wait. We can do the two reports at once, which is handy.'

During this time I was shut in a little office adjoining the governor's. I was left on my own there, behind a well-bolted door.

I do not know what I was thinking about, or for how long I had been there, when sudden raucous laughter in my ear aroused me from my daydream.

Trembling, I looked up. I was no longer alone in the cell. A man was there with me, a man of about fifty-five, of medium height and stocky build, wrinkled, stooped and greying, with a shifty look in his grey eyes and a twisted sneer on his face. He was dirty, ragged, half-naked, and repulsive to behold.

It appears that the door had opened, disgorged him, and then closed again before I had noticed. If only death could come like this!

For a few seconds the man and I stared at one another, he keeping up this rattling laugh, and I half bemused and half afraid.

'What are you doing here?' I then asked him.

'What does it look like?' he replied. 'The bleeding *limbo*, that's what.'

'The limbo! Whatever does that mean?'

This question only increased his amusement. 'It means,' he coughed out through his fit of mirth, 'that blade runner will score a basket with my dreaming spire in six weeks. Yer nut will be off your shoulders in six hours, so that'll make two. Ha, ha! I can see that the penny's beginning to drop.'

Indeed I had gone pale, and my hair was standing on end. It was the other condemned man, who had been sentenced today and was bound for the cell at Bicêtre that I had bequeathed to him.

He went on, 'Here's my story, for what it's worth. I'm the son of a clever crook; but as ill luck would have it, old *Charlie* did his tie up for him one day. This was in the days when the gallows ruled, by the grace of God. So at six I had no father or mother; in summer I turned cartwheels in the dust on the highway, so that people would throw me a penny from the windows of the coaches; in winter I went barefoot in the mud, blowing on my frozen fingers; you could see my legs through my trousers. When I was nine, I began to rely on me *mitts*; now and then I liberated a wallet, or *half-inched a coat*; at ten, I was a promising young *dip*. Then I fell in with some good mates, and by seventeen, I was a *regular tea-leaf*. I could *jemmy* a shop door, or cut a *Jenny Lea*. But I was catched, and not too young to take an oar in the *junior navy*. The galleys are tough: you sleep on a board, drink water, eat black bread, and drag a frigging great ball behind you: the sun beats down on you, and so do the screws. They crop you, too, and I had such lovely brown hair. Anyway, I served my time. Fifteen years of sheer murder! I was thirty-two. One fine morning, I was given my travel papers and sixty-six francs that I had saved over fifteen years in the galleys, working sixteen hours a day, thirty days a month, and twelve months a year. Even so, I wanted to go straight with my sixty-six francs, and an honest heart beat beneath these rags, which is more than you could say about some *padres in their frocks*. But that bastard passport! it was yellow, and on it was written, "Freed convict." I had to show it wherever I went, and present it every week to the mayor of the village where I was made to *doss*. Some reference, eh? a blooming convict! So people were afraid of me, children ran off, and doors were slammed in my face. Nobody would give me work, and my sixty-six francs soon ran out. After that, I had to live. I was strong and not afraid of a bit of hard work, but nobody wanted to know. I offered to work for fifteen sous a day, for ten, or for five. No dice. What was I to do? One day, I was hungry. I stove in a baker's window with my elbow and grabbed a loaf of bread, but the baker grabbed me. I didn't get to eat the bread, but I got hard labour for life, with three letters branded on my shoulder. You can see them if you like. The lawyers call this a subsequent offence. So now I'm an *old lag*. Back to Toulon again, but this time with the *greencaps*. I had to escape. To do that, I only had three walls to tunnel through and two chains to file, but still, I had a nail. So I escaped. The warning cannon was fired; for we lags are like the cardinals of Rome, dressed in red[11], and the gun goes off when we leave. They missed by a mile. This time I didn't have a yellow passport, but I didn't have any money either. I met some mates who had served their time too, or been sprung. Their *guv'nor* asked me would I fancy *spilling a drop of plonk on the pavement*? I signed on, and started to kill for a living. Sometimes it was a stagecoach, sometimes a mail-coach, and sometimes a cattle dealer on horseback. We took the money, let the mount or the vehicle go on its way, and buried the man beneath a tree, making sure that his feet didn't stick out; then we danced on the grave to stamp the earth down again. So that's how I've spent my life, bivvying in the bushes, kipping in the open air, hunted from pillar to post, but free and my own man. It's all one, and there comes an end to everything. One night the *cuff brigade* took us in their trap. My *oppos* all scarpered, but I'm getting a bit old to run fast, and the posh hats nabbed me. I was brought here, just one step from the bottom of the ladder. Stealing a handkerchief or killing a man made no odds now, because I had reoffended... again. It was the *grim reaper* for me, all right. My fate was soon signed and sealed. To tell you the truth, I was getting too old and too clumsy. My father *got hitched to a widow*, and they're doing out my cell in *Mount-with-bad-Grace Priory*. End of story, pal.'

I had stood dumbly listening to him. He started laughing more loudly even than before, and tried to take my hand. I drew back in horror.

'Look here, my friend,' he said to me, 'I must say you don't look too chipper. Now *keep a tight arsehole* when it comes to your turn. You get stage fright when you're due to tread the boards, but you soon get into the swing of things! I wish I was there to show you the ropes. By Christ! I've a good mind not to appeal, if they'll top me today along with you. The same priest will do for both of us; I don't mind eating off your plate. You can't say fairer than that. Aren't I a good mate to you? Is it a deal, eh, pal?'

He took another step, drawing nearer to me.

'Sir,' I replied, pushing him away, 'I thank you, but no.'

Renewed laughter at my reply. 'Oh, sir is it? Oh, we're a *toff*, are we? That's all I need: a toff!'

I cut in, 'My friend, I need to gather my thoughts; please leave me alone.'

My serious tone made him suddenly thoughtful. He nodded his greying, almost bald head as he scratched at his bare, hairy chest beneath his open shirt. 'The *sky pilot*'s been at him,' he muttered under his breath, 'say no more.' A few moments' silence, then, 'All right,' he said to me almost timidly, 'toff or no toff, you've a good coat there going begging! Old blade runner will whip it as soon as look at it. Give us it here, and I can sell it for some tobacco.'

I took off my frock-coat and gave it to him. He started to clap his hands, like an excited child. But then, seeing me down to my shirt and shivering, 'Sir, you're cold, put this on; it's raining and you'd get wet. Anyway, you want to look good on the cart.'

As he spoke, he took off his jacket of coarse grey wool and helped me into it. I submitted passively.

Then I went over and leaned against the wall, dumbfounded by this man's behaviour. He had begun to examine the coat I had given him, and would not stop shouting for joy.

'The pockets are like new! The collar's hardly worn! I'll get at least fifteen francs for it. What a stroke of luck! Tobacco to last me six weeks.'

The door opened once more. They came for us both: I was to go to the room where the condemned men wait until it is time, and he to Bicêtre. Still laughing, he took his place between the members of his escort, saying to the gendarmes, 'Don't get it wrong, now; Monsieur and I may have swapped coats, but I'll thank you not to take me instead of him. Hell! that would be a fine cock-up, just when I've got my baccy money!'

24

The disgusting old reprobate has taken my coat, for I hardly gave it to him, and left me this rag, his disgusting jacket. What am I going to look like?

It was not out of indifference or a feeling of charity that I let him take it. No, but because he was stronger than I was. If I had refused, he could have beaten me to a pulp.

And charity was furthest from my mind! I was full of ill will. I wish I could have strangled him with my bare hands, the old thief!

and trampled him underfoot!

I feel my heart full of rage and bitterness. I think that my sac of bile has burst. Death turns you nasty.

25

They took me to a cell with four bare walls and, needless to say, many bars on the window and bolts on the door.

I asked for a table, a chair, and writing materials. All of these were brought to me.

Then I requested a bed. The warder looked at me with astonishment, as if to say, 'What's the point?'

Even so, they set up a trestle bed in the corner. But at the same time, a gendarme was posted in what they call *my room*. Are they genuinely worried that with the help of the mattress I can do away with myself?

26

It is ten o'clock.

Oh, my poor little girl! Six more hours and I shall be dead! I shall be something disgusting left lying on the slab of the lecture theatre; at one end, a mould will be taken of the head, and at the other, the body will be dissected. Then a coffin will be filled with what is left, and proceed to Clamart.

That is what will be done to your father by men, none of whom hate me, all of whom feel sorry for me and could save me. They are going to kill me. Can you understand that, Marie? kill me in cold blood, in solemn ceremony, for the edification of the public! Great God in heaven!

Poor little girl! your father who loved you so, your father who kissed the fair skin on your little neck, who never tired of running his hand through your silken curls, who would cup your pretty round face in his hands, who dandled you on his knee, and each evening joined your little hands together in prayer!

Who will do all this for you now? Who will love you? All the children of your age will have fathers, except you. My child, how will you learn not to expect New Year presents, fine toys, sweets, and kisses? How, poor orphan, will you learn to do without food and drink?

Oh! if the jurors had only seen her, my pretty little Marie! Then they would have understood that you do not kill the father of a child of three.

And when she grows up, if she lives until then, what will become of her? Her father will be of notorious memory in Paris. She will be ashamed of me and my name; she will be despised, rejected, and vilified because of me, when I love her more than all the world. Oh, little Marie whom I love so much! Is it true that you will feel shame and loathing for me?

It is my wretched fault! What a crime I have committed, and what a crime I am forcing society to commit!

Oh! can it be true that I shall die before the end of the day? Can it really be me? The muffled shouts that I hear outside, the gleeful spectators already swarming along the embankments, the gen-darmes getting ready in their barracks, the black-gowned priest, and the other man with the red hands, all of it is for me! For *I* am to die, the man here present, living, moving, breathing, and sitting at this table, which is like any other table and could just as easily be somewhere else. It is all for me, this person whom I can touch and whose feelings I share, and whose clothes hang on me like this!

27

If only I knew how it is done, and in what way you die upon it! But it's dreadful, for I do not.

The name of the thing is appalling, and I have no idea how until now I was able to write it and to speak it.

The way these ten letters combine, their expression and their outward appearance are propitious to horrid imaginings, and the wretched doctor who invented the apparatus had a predestined name[12].

The image that I attach to this hideous word is all the more distressing for being vague and indeterminate. Each syllable is like a part of the machine, whose monstrous framework is being built and dismantled unceasingly in my mind.

I dare not ask any questions about it, but it is terrible not to know what it is like, or how to behave. It seems that there is a swinging-plank, and that you are laid flat on your stomach ... Oh! my hair will turn white before my head falls!

28

And yet I did catch a glimpse of it once.

One day, I was crossing the Place de Grève in a carriage, at about eleven in the morning. The vehicle suddenly stopped.

There was a crowd on the square. I put my head out of the window. A mob was packed into La Grève and lining the embankment, and men, women, and children were standing on the parapet. Above their heads you could see a sort of red wooden dais being erected by three men.

A man was to be executed that day, and they were building the machine.

I turned my head away before seeing it all. By the side of my carriage, a woman was saying to a child, 'Why, look! the blade isn't falling smoothly and they're going to grease the track with a bit of candle.'

That is probably where they are up to today. It has just struck eleven. They will be greasing the track.

But this time, you poor devil, you will not turn your head away!

29

My pardon, oh, my pardon! For they may pardon me. The king bears me no ill will. Let my counsel be sent for, quickly, my counsel! I consent to the galleys. Five years' hard labour should be sufficient; or twenty years; or branding, then penal servitude for life. But spare me my life.

Convicts are free at least to walk about, and see the sun.

The priest came back.

He has white hair, a kindly manner, and a good and honest face; for indeed he is a fine and compassionate man. This morning I saw him empty his purse into the hands of the prisoners. Why is it, then, that his voice shows no emotion and kindles none? Why is it that he has not yet said anything to me that moved my reason or my heart?

This morning, I was in a daze. I hardly heard what he said to me. Yet his words seemed useless, and left me feeling indifferent; they slid by like the cold raindrops now falling on this icy pane.

Yet when just now he came back to keep me company, I was cheered to see him. Among all these men, I thought, he is the only one who is still a human being to me. And I thirsted avidly for good and consoling words.

We sat down, he on the chair and I on the bed. He began, 'My son…' This word went straight to my heart. He then went on, 'My son, do you believe in God?'

'Yes, Father,' I replied.

'Do you believe in the holy Catholic, apostolic, and Roman church?'

'With all my heart,' I said.

'My son,' he went on, 'you seem to lack conviction.'

Then he began to speak. He spoke at length; he uttered many words; then, when he thought he had said enough, he got up and looked at me for the first time since the beginning of his speech, asking me, 'Well?'

I swear that I had listened to him raptly at first, then attentively, then courteously.

I too stood up. 'Sir,' I replied, 'leave me alone, I beg you.'

He asked me, 'When shall I come again?'

'I shall let you know.'

Then he went out, not angrily, but nodding his head as if he were saying to himself, 'A heathen!'

No, however low I may have fallen, I am not a heathen, and God is my witness that I believe in Him. But what did this old man say to me? There was nothing that was felt, nothing pitying, nothing born of his tears, nothing torn from his soul, nothing going from his heart to mine, nothing given by him to me. Instead of this, it was perniciously vague, applicable to everything and everybody; rhetorical where gravity was required, clichéd when simplicity was needed: what you would call an emotive sermon or theological lament. Here and there it was spiced with a quotation in Latin from Saint Augustine, or maybe from Saint Gregory. In any case, he appeared to be repeating a passage delivered twenty times already, going parrot-fashion over a topic so well known it was seemingly erased from his memory. His eyes made no contact, his voice was neutral, and his hands made no movement.

Yet how could it be otherwise? This priest is the official chaplain to the prison. His role is to console and to urge repentance, and he makes a living from it. His eloquence is lavished on convicts and the condemned. He confesses and accompanies them because it is his job. He has grown old leading men to their deaths. He has long been hardened to what makes others tremble; his powdered white hair no longer stands on end; the hulks and the scaffold are everyday occurrences to him. He is indifferent. No doubt he has written out a page in his notebook for convicts, and another for men condemned to death. The day before, he is notified that somebody will require his ministrations at such and such a time; he asks whether it is to be a convict or a guillotine victim, glances over the appropriate page, then along he comes. So it falls out that those bound for Toulon or La Grève are in a common place for him, and that he is a commonplace for them.

Oh! instead of this, run and fetch me some young curate, some old priest, taken from any parish at all; go and find him at his fireside, where he is reading his breviary, not expecting to be disturbed, and say to him: 'A man is about to die, and you are the one who must bring him comfort. You must be with him when his hands are tied, and when his hair is cut; you must get into the cart with him and hold your crucifix up between him and the executioner; you must be jolted with him over the cobbles on the trip to La Grève; with him you must fight your way through the horrible, bloodthirsty crowd; you must embrace him at the foot of the scaffold, and stay until the head is here and the body over there.'

So bring me this man, trembling and shivering from head to foot; let me fall into his arms or down at his knees; he will weep and we shall weep, he will be eloquent and I shall be comforted, and my heart shall melt into his, and he will take my soul, and I his God.

But what is this kindly old gentleman to me? and what am I to him? Just one more member of the race of unfortunates, one more shade to go with the many he has seen, one more figure to add to his total of executions.

Perhaps I am wrong to reject him like this, for it is he that is good and I that am bad. Alas! it is not my fault. My breath stinks of the scaffold, and blasts and withers everything.

They have just brought food in to me, thinking that I could do with some. It was beautifully cooked and served, chicken, I suppose, with something or other. I tried hard to eat, but the very first mouthful dropped from my lips, so bitter and foul it all seemed.

31

A gentleman wearing a hat just came in, who barely looked at me before opening out a boxwood rule and starting to take vertical measurements of the stones in the walls, saying loudly to himself, *That's fine*, or, *Can't be right*.

I asked the gendarme who he was. Apparently he is some sort of architect's assistant employed by the prison.

He in turn began to grow curious about me. He exchanged a few monosyllables with the turnkey who was escorting him; then he glanced at me, tossed his head casually, and carried on talking loudly and taking measurements.

When his work was over, he came up to me and said in a booming voice, 'My dear friend, in six months' time this prison will be much improved.' By which he seemed to imply, 'But unfortunately not for your benefit.'

He was almost smiling. I thought that soon he would begin to joke with me knowingly, the way that a bride is teased on her wedding night.

My gendarme, an old soldier with stripes, took the reply out of my mouth, 'Sir,' he told him, 'you should keep your voice down and have some respect for the dead.'

The architect left.

I stood there like one of the stones he had been measuring.

32

And then something scarcely believable was to occur.

My kindly old gendarme went off duty, and like an ungrateful wretch I did not even shake him by the hand. He was replaced by another, a man with a receding forehead, bovine eyes, and a vacant expression.

Not that I had paid any attention to this. I had my back to the door, and was sitting at the table, laying my hand on my brow to try to cool it, lost in troubled thought.

A soft tap on my shoulder made me turn round. It was the relief constable, with whom I was on my own.

This is more or less the way he spoke to me.

'Prisoner, are you a decent sort?'

'No,' I told him.

He seemed taken aback by the abruptness of my reply, yet hesitantly continued, 'Nobody is wicked for the fun of it.'

'Why not?' I replied. 'If you've got nothing more to say to me, then leave me alone. Come on, spit it out.'

'Beg pardon, my prisoner,' he replied. 'A few words in your ear. If you could make a poor man happy at no cost to yourself, would you not do so?'

I shrugged my shoulders. 'Have you got a slate loose? I'm a pretty unlikely source of happiness. How would *I* make anybody happy?'

With an enigmatic look scarce in keeping with his dumb countenance, he lowered his voice and said, 'Yes, my prisoner, yes you bring happiness, and yes you bring fortune. It will all come to me from you. Let me tell you how. I am a poor constable. My duties are heavy, and my pay is meagre; the upkeep of my horse alone is costing me a mint. So I play the lottery, to even things up. You need to make ends meet. So far I've been close to winning, but you need good numbers. I look high and low for good ones, but never hit on the right combination. I play the 76, and the 77 is drawn. I stick with the same ones, but they never come out. Be patient, please, I'm coming to the point. Which is that you are a winner for me. Excuse me for saying so, prisoner, but I'm told that your turn has come today. And it's certain that dead men who have been executed can see the coming lottery numbers. So why not promise to come back tomorrow evening with three numbers for me, three good ones. Would you mind? Don't worry, I'm not afraid of ghosts. Here's my address: Popincourt barracks, stairway A, room 26, at the end of the corridor. You'll remember me, won't you? You can even come this evening, if you'd rather.'

I would not have bothered to reply to this clown if a gleam of crazy hope had not suddenly shot through my mind. My present situation was so desperate that sometimes you believe that you could split a chain with a hair.

'Listen,' I said to him, hamming it as much as can be expected of a man about to die, 'in point of fact I can make you richer than the King, make you win millions. But on one condition.'

He gaped wide-eyed at me. 'What is it? what is it? anything you say, my prisoner.'

'I promise you not three numbers but four, if you will change clothes with me.'

'Is that all!' he cried, undoing the first hooks on his uniform with alacrity.

I had got up from my chair. I was watching his every movement, and my heart beat madly. Already I saw doors being opened to the gendarme in uniform, and the square, and the street, and the Palais de Justice in the distance behind me!

But then he turned round in puzzlement. 'Hold on! It's not so that you can escape?'

I realised that all was lost. Yet I made one totally futile and mad last attempt!

'Of course,' I told him, 'but you will have made a fortune.'

He cut in, 'Not on your life! What about my numbers? For them to be good, you have to be dead.'

I sat down again, silent and crushed more completely by all the hope that had just been extinguished.

33

I closed my eyes, put my hands over them, and tried to bury the present in the past. While I daydream, the memories of my childhood and youth return one after the other; they are gentle, calm, and happy, like islands of flowers floating above the inky depths of confused thoughts that spin around my brain.

I see myself as a child once more, a laughing and innocent schoolboy, playing, running, and shouting with my brothers on the central walk of that wild, green garden where my first years were spent. It belonged to a former convent, whose leaden roof looks down on the dark dome of the Val-de-Grâce.

And four years on, I see myself again, still a child, but already dreamy and passionate. There is a girl in the secluded garden.

It is the little Spanish girl with big eyes and long hair, brown, golden skin, red lips, and pink cheeks, fourteen-year-old Pepa from Andalusia[13].

Our mothers told us to run along there: but we went to walk.

We were told to play, but as children of the same age yet of different sex, we talk.

It was not a year ago, though, that we ran and tumbled together. I squabbled with Pepita over the biggest apple on the tree, and hit her because of a bird's nest. She cried, and I said, 'Serves you right!' Then we both ran and told tales to our mothers, who told us pointedly not to be so stupid, but thought privately that we were right.

Now she is leaning on my arm, and I am so proud and excited. We walk slowly, and speak in low voices. She drops her handkerchief; I pick it up. Our hands tremble as they touch. She talks to me of the little birds, of the star that is shining in the distance, of the rosy sunset seen behind the trees, or perhaps about

73

her boarding-school friends, her dress, and her ribbons. We say innocent things that make us both blush. The girl has become a young woman.

That evening – it was a summer evening – we were under the chestnut trees at the bottom of the garden. After one of the long silences that punctuated our walks, she suddenly let go of my arm and said, 'Come on, let's run!'

I can see her now, she was dressed in black, in mourning for her grandmother. A childish idea occurred to her, turning Pepa back into Pepita, and she challenged me, 'Let's run!'

So she ran off in front of me, her waist as slender as a bee's and her little feet kicking her dress up to mid-calf. I ran after her, and she ran on, with the wind she whipped up lifting her black cape now and then, and showing me her lithe, brown back.

I was quite maddened. Catching up with her near the broken-down old well, I grabbed hold of her belt, which meant that I had won, and made her sit down on a grassy bank; she offered no resistance. She was breathless and laughing. But I was serious, and gazed through her black lashes into her black eyes.

'Sit down here,' she said. 'It is still light, and we can read something. Have you got a book?'

I had with me the second volume of *Voyages* of Spallanzani[14]. I opened it at random, moved closer to her, she leaned her shoulder on mine, and both of us began to read the same page quietly to ourselves. Before turning over, she always had to wait for me. My brain was less nimble than hers.

'Have you finished?' she would say to me, when I had hardly begun.

Meanwhile our heads touched, our hair intermingled, our mouths breathed closer together, and suddenly met.

When we tried to carry on reading, stars were twinkling in the sky.

'Oh! Mummy, Mummy,' she said when she went back in, 'you can't imagine how far we ran!'

But I kept silent.

'You're very quiet,' said my mother. 'You look sad.'

Yet my heart was in paradise.

That evening is one I shall remember all my life.

All my life!

34

The clock has just struck, some hour or other, for I can hardly hear the strokes. I feel as though there is an organ playing between my ears: it is my last thoughts reverberating.

When I seek this final refuge in my memories, my crime looms up and I am horrified, but I should like to be more repentant. I felt more remorse before I was sentenced; since then, it seems that there is room for none but thoughts of death. And yet I should like to show full repentance.

When I have dwelt for a while on what is past in my life, and then return to the axe blow that must end it shortly, I shiver as if it were something unexpected. My sweet childhood! my sweet adolescence! they are a gold fabric with a bloodied hem. Between then and now runs a river of blood, the victim's and mine.

If one day my story is read, it will seem incredible that so many years of innocence are followed by this abominable year, beginning with crime and ending with punishment; it will seem not to respect the sequence.

And yet, O wretched laws and wretched men, I was not an evil man!

Oh! that I must die in a few hours, remembering that a year ago, on a day such as this, I was free and innocent, walking beneath the trees and kicking up the autumn leaves.

35

At this very moment, in all the houses built round the Palais and La Grève, and throughout Paris, men are coming and going quite freely, talking and laughing, reading the paper and thinking about business, shopkeepers are selling, young women are getting their ball gowns ready for this evening, and mothers are playing with their children.

36

I remember that one day, as a boy, I went to see the great bell of Notre-Dame.

I was already giddy from climbing the dark, spiral staircase and crossing the narrow walkway between the two towers, over Paris stretched beneath my feet, when I entered the cage of stone and wood where hang the half-ton bell and its clapper.

I tiptoed gingerly over the uneven boards, gazing from a distance on the bell so revered by the children and people of Paris, not a little afraid to find that the sloping slate awnings which surround the bell tower ran down from the level of my feet. Through the gaps I had almost a bird's eye view of the cathedral square, with passers-by the size of ants.

Suddenly the giant bell rang, and a deep, surging vibration ran through the air, and made the massive tower shake. The floor banged up and down on the joists. The noise almost knocked me backwards; I staggered, nearly falling and sliding down the sloping slates. Panic-stricken, I lay on the floorboards, clinging tightly on with both arms, speechless and breathless from the awesome dinning into my ears, while my eyes looked down over a precipice to the square so far below, where people I envied went peacefully by.

Well, then! I seem still to be in the bell tower. I am dazed and bedazzled all at once. A great bell tolls through the recesses of my brain, and I look around and see that calm and peaceful life I have left behind, and in which other men may still walk free, from afar across a yawning void.

37

The Hôtel de Ville is a forbidding building.

With its steeply sloping roof, its rococo pinnacles, its big white clock-face, its column motifs on each floor, its thousand windows, its steps worn down by footprints, and its two arches to the right and to the left, it stands there on a dead level with La Grève, dark, gloomy, its face pock-marked with age, and so black that it reflects sunlight back.

On execution days, it disgorges gendarmes from its every door, and watches the condemned man from its every window.

And in the evening, its clock-face, which told the fatal hour, glows luminous on its grim façade.

38

It is a quarter past one.

These are my sensations at present:

A splitting headache. My back is cold, and my forehead burning. Each time I get up or lean over, it seems that there is a liquid floating around in my head that dashes my brain against the walls of the skull.

I shake convulsively, and now and then the pen falls from my fingers, as if jolted by a galvanic shock.

My eyes burn as though I was surrounded by smoke.

My elbows are tender.

Two hours and forty-five minutes to go, and I shall be cured.

39

They say there's nothing to it, that you don't feel pain, that it's a merciful release, and that in this way death is made easy.

Is that so? Then what about this six-week death agony and this day-long death rattle? What about the mental torment endured through this fateful day that passes so slowly and so fast? And what about the rising scale of tortures ending with the scaffold?

This is not suffering, apparently.

Whether blood runs out drop by drop, or the intellect dies thought by thought, are they not the same final spasms?

Anyway, how can they be sure that it's painless? Who told them that? Since when did a decapitated head stand up on the rim of the basket and shout to the people, 'I didn't feel a thing'?

And did any of their victims ever come back to thank them, saying, 'It's a fine invention. Couldn't be bettered. It works to perfection'?

Did Robespierre ever? Did Louis XVI?

But no, nothing! less than a minute, less than a second, and the deed is done. Have they ever placed themselves, even mentally in the position of one lying there, at the instant when the heavy, falling blade bites into the flesh, sections the nerves, and breaks the bones...

Come now, half a second is all it takes! and pain must be minimal...

How appalling!

40

It is strange, but I never stop thinking about the King. However much I shake my head and try to ignore it, a voice in my ear keeps saying:

'In this very city, at this very hour, and not very far from here, there lives in another palace a man who also has guards on every door, a man set aside like you from the common herd, the only difference being that he is as high above it as you are beneath. Every minute of his life is devoted to the pursuit of glory, greatness, pleasure, and rapture. Around him all is love, respect, and veneration. The loudest voices are lowered when speaking to him, and the proudest wills must bend. He has nothing meaner than silk and gold before his eyes. At this very moment, he will be conducting a council of ministers in which everybody agrees with him; or maybe he is thinking of tomorrow's hunting or this evening's ball, certain that the festivities will begin on time, with others preparing his enjoyment for him. Well, this man is made of flesh and blood like you! And for the horrible scaffold to collapse in a heap, for you to be given back life, liberty, fortune, and family, he would only have to take this pen and write the seven letters of his name[15] at the bottom of a piece of paper, or the paths of his carriage and your cart would only have to cross. And he is good, and might well wish for nothing better, yet it will never happen!'

41

So let us deal courageously with death, taking the dread prospect in our two hands and staring it in the face. Let us ask it to explain what it is, know what it requires of us, and look at it from every angle, spelling out the riddle and peering forward into the grave.

I feel that no sooner have my eyes been shut than they will be suffused with brightness, and my mind will journey endlessly through chasms of light. I feel that the sky will glow with its own luminosity, that stars will be dark speckles, and instead of being golden spangles on black velvet, as they are for living eyes, will appear like black spots on a cloth of gold.

But knowing my wretched luck, I might find it an ugly, deep void, its walls clad in darkness, down through which I shall fall forever, past shapes that move in the gloom.

Or perhaps I shall awaken after the blow to find myself on some flat and slimy surface, on hands and knees in the darkness and turning round and round like a head as it rolls. With a high wind at my back, and buffeted every so often by other rolling heads. There will be puddles in places, with streams of a warm, unfamiliar liquid; and all will be black. When my eyes swivel upwards, they will behold nothing but a pitch-black sky, its heavy layers bearing down on them, and in the far distance will loom up great arches of smoke that is blacker than the darkness. Tiny red sparks hovering in the night will turn into birds of fire as they draw closer. And thus it will be for all eternity.

Perhaps too, on dark winter nights at fixed dates, the dead of La Grève will gather together on this, their square. I shall not fail to be present in the pale, bloody crowd. There will be no moon, and the voices will be whispers. The Hôtel de Ville will be there, with its crumbling façade, its ragged roof, and its clock whose hands move mercilessly on for us all. On the square will be a guillotine from hell, on which a devil will behead an executioner. It will be four in the morning, and our turn to throng round.

All this I do anticipate. But if these dead return, in what form do they return? What do they keep of their incomplete and mutilated body? What do they choose? Does the head or the body turn into a ghost?

Alas! what does death do to our souls? in what form do *they* reappear? what is subtracted from or added to them? where do they inhabit? can they ever be lent eyes of flesh, to look down on earth and weep?

Fetch me a priest! a priest who can answer my questions! I need a priest, and a crucifix to kiss!

Oh, God! It is still the same man!

42

I asked him to let me sleep, and threw myself on the bed.

My head was so congested with blood that I did in fact manage to sleep. My last sleep of this kind.

I had a dream.

I dreamed that it was night. I seemed to be in my study with two or three friends. I don't remember which.

My wife was in bed next door, sleeping with her child.

My friends and I were talking in low voices, and were terrified by what we said.

Suddenly, I felt I heard a noise in one of the other rooms. A faint, strange, and unidentifiable noise.

My friends had also heard it. We listened: it was like a lock being quietly turned, or a bolt being surreptitiously sawn through.

There was something about it that chilled us: we were afraid. The hour was so late we thought thieves might have broken in.

We decided to go and see. I got up and took the candle. My friends followed me one by one.

We went through the bedroom next door. My wife was sleeping with her child.

Next came the drawing-room. Nothing there. The portraits stared at us from their gold frames on the red drapes. It seemed to me that the door leading from the drawing-room to the dining-room was not in its usual position.

We entered the dining-room, and walked round it. I led the way. The door leading onto the stairs was locked and bolted, as were the windows. When I got near the stove, I saw that the linen cupboard was open, and that the door of this cupboard was pulled over the corner of the wall as if to hide it.

I found that odd. We thought that somebody was behind the door.

I put my hand on the door, and tried to close the cupboard; it did not budge. I was surprised and pulled harder, whereupon it suddenly gave way to reveal a little old lady, standing quite still, as if glued to the corner of the room, with her eyes closed and her hands hanging open.

There was something eerie about it, and even to think of it makes my hair stand on end.

I asked the old woman, 'What are you doing here?'

She made no reply.

I asked her, 'Who are you?'

She did not reply, did not move, and her eyes remained closed.

My friends said, 'She must be an accomplice of the gang of thieves; they ran off when they heard us coming, but her escape was blocked and she hid here.'

I questioned her again, but she remained silent, motionless and unseeing.

One of us tried to push her over, and she fell.

She fell stiffly, like a piece of wood or a dead thing.

We prodded her with our feet, then two of us lifted her back up and leaned her once more against the wall. She gave no sign of life. We shouted in her ear, but she stayed so silent that she could have been deaf.

By now we were losing patience, and there was a note of anger in our terror. One of my friends said, 'Play the candle under her chin.'

I waved the lighted wick beneath her chin. At this, she half-opened one eye, an eye that was blank, dull, hideous, and unseeing.

I removed the flame, and said, 'About time, too! Will you speak, you old witch? Who are you?'

The eye closed again, as if of its own accord.

'Now she has gone too far,' said the others. 'Give her the candle again! and again! she will have to talk.'

Once more I passed the flame under the old woman's chin.

And then she opened her two eyes slowly, her gaze swept round us all, and, bending down swiftly, she blew out the candle with her icy breath. Just at that moment, in the darkness below, I felt three sharp teeth biting into my hand.

I woke up, shivering and drenched in cold sweat.

The good chaplain was sitting at the foot of my bed, reading his prayer book.

'Did I sleep for long?' I asked him.

'My son,' he said to me, 'you slept for an hour. We brought your child to see you. She is waiting for you in the next room. I told them not to wake you.'

'Oh!' I cried, 'let me see my daughter!'

43

She is young, she is rosy-cheeked, she has big eyes, she is just beautiful!

She is wearing a little dress that suits her so well.

I took her and swung her up in my arms, sat her on my knee, and kissed her hair.

But why did her mother not come? Mother is ill, and so is grandmother. Just as I thought.

She looked at me with some surprise, allowing herself to be stroked, hugged, and smothered with kisses, but looking anxiously from time to time towards her maid, who sat weeping in the corner.

At last I managed to speak. 'Marie,' I said, 'my little Marie.'

I clasped her fiercely to my sobbing breast. She gave a faint cry. 'Oh, sir, you are hurting me,' she said.

Sir! It is nearly a year since she saw me, poor child. She has forgotten my face, my speech, and my tone of voice; and who else would recognise me with this beard, these clothes, and this pallid complexion? Have I already been wiped clean from her memory, the only one in which I had wished to live on! And am I no longer a father! no longer worthy to be called *daddy* – that child's word too pretty for the adult to use!

Yet I would have gladly given the forty years of life I am losing to hear it once more from her mouth, just one more time.

'Now Marie,' I said to her, clasping her tiny hands in mine, 'don't you know who I am?'

She looked at me with her pretty eyes, and replied, 'Why, no.'

'Look carefully,' I repeated. 'Don't tell me you don't know who I am?'

'Oh, yes,' she said. 'A gentleman.'

Alas! how tragic it is to love but one person in the whole world, with all your heart, and for her to be there, seeing and looking at you, speaking and replying to you, yet not knowing you! To seek consolation from her alone, yet she is the only one not to know that it is because you are going to die!

'Marie,' I went on, 'do you have a daddy?'

'Yes, sir,' the child said.

'Well, where is he?'

She looked up, blinking wide in astonishment. 'Why, don't you know? He is dead.'

Then she cried out, for I had almost dropped her.

'Dead!' I said. 'Marie, do you know what it means to be dead?'

'Yes, sir,' she replied. 'He is in the ground and also in heaven.' She went on, unprompted, 'Every morning and evening, I sit on mummy's knee and pray for him.'

I kissed her on the forehead. 'Marie, let me hear you pray.'

'Oh no, sir. You can't say prayers during the day. Come to my house this evening, and you can hear me.'

That was quite enough, and I broke in, 'Marie, I am your daddy.'

'Oh!' she said.

I added, 'Do you want me for your daddy?'

The child turned away. 'No, my daddy was much more handsome.'

I showered her with tears and with kisses. She tried to wriggle free from my arms, crying, 'You're scratching me with your beard.'

Then I sat her back on my knee, staring tenderly at her, and asked her, 'Marie, can you read?'

'Yes,' she replied. 'I'm a good reader. Mummy helps me with my spelling.'

'Let's hear you read something,' I asked her, pointing to a screwed-up piece of paper she was holding in one of her little hands.

She shook her pretty head. 'Oh, no! I can only read fairy stories.'

'Please try, for me. Go on, read.'

She unfolded the paper, and began to spell out with her finger,

'S.E.N., *sen*, T.E.N.C.E., *tence*, SENTENCE…'

I tore it from her hands. She was reading out my death sentence to me. Her maid had bought the sheet for a penny. It was costing me a good deal more.

Words are inadequate to describe what I felt. My rough behaviour had frightened her, and she was nearly crying. Then suddenly, she said, 'Give me back my paper, will you! I want to play with it.'

I gave her back to the maid, saying, 'Take her away.'

And I flopped back onto my chair, dismal, alone and desperate. Now would be a good time for them to come: all my ties are unbound, and the last string of my heart is broken. I am ready for whatever they will do to me.

44

The priest is a kindly man, and so is the gendarme. I am sure they shed a tear when I asked for my child to be taken away.

It's over. Now I must steel my courage and be resolute when I think of the executioner, the cart, the gendarmes, the crowd, and of what has been built for me on that deathly Place de Grève, which could be cobbled with all the heads it has seen fall.

I think I have one more hour to get ready for all this.

45

All the people will laugh, clap their hands, and shout hurrah. Yet among all these free men who have never fallen foul of gaolers and who hurry eagerly to see an execution, among this mass of heads crammed into the square, more than one will be predestined, sooner or later, to follow mine into the red basket. More than one who comes here on my account will later come on his own.

For these fated beings, at a certain spot on the Place de Grève there is a lethal spot, a magnetic pole, a trap. And they circle round it till it gobbles them up.

46

My little Marie! She has gone off to play again; she can see the crowd through the cab window, and has already forgotten this *gentleman.*

I wonder if I still have time to write a few pages for her, so that one day she may read them, and fifteen years hence, weep for today.

Yes, I must be the one to tell her my story, and explain why the name I have given her is stained with blood.

47

MY STORY

Publisher's note: *The sheets that were joined to this have so far not been found. Perhaps, as those that follow would seem to indicate, the condemned man did not have time to write them. The idea did occur to him rather late.*

48

From a room in the Hôtel de Ville

From the Hôtel de Ville!... Yes, here I am at last. The dreadful journey is over. The square is down below, and beneath my window the ghoulish spectators stand and wait, yelping and cackling.

Try as I would to steel and tense my sinews, I felt my heart sink. When I saw above the heads those two red posts topped by the black triangle, standing between the two lamps on the embankment, I must say that my heart sank. I asked to make a last statement. I was brought up here, and they have gone off to fetch some attorney. I am waiting for him, and have won some breathing space.

Now, where was I?

The clock struck three, and they came to tell me that it was time. I shuddered, almost as though my mind had been on other things for the last six hours, six weeks, or six months. For it did seem unexpected.

They led me along their corridors and down their stairs. They made me wait between two of the gatehouses, in a dark, narrow, and vaulted room into which the rainy, foggy daylight hardly penetrated. There was a chair in the middle. I was told to sit down, and I sat.

A few people were standing by the door and along the walls, as were the priest, the gendarmes, and then three other men.

The first, the tallest and most senior, was stout and red-faced. He was wearing a frock-coat and a battered tricorn hat. He was the man.

It was the executioner, the guillotine's auxiliary. The two others were servants to him.

Hardly had I sat down than the other two crept catlike up on me from behind, and I suddenly felt the kiss of cold steel on my hair, and the squeaking of scissors in my ears.

Locks of my roughly cropped hair fell onto my shoulders, and the man in the tricorn hat brushed them gently off with his big hand.

The people standing round were speaking in an undertone.

There was a great noise outside, like a rustling vibration in the air. First of all, I thought it was the river; but when laughter broke out, I realised it was the crowd.

A young man sitting by the window, who was writing in pencil in a pocketbook, asked one of the gaolers what this operation was called.

'The toilette of the condemned,' the other replied.

I gathered that it would be in tomorrow's newspaper.

Suddenly, one of the assistants stripped off my jacket, and the other took hold of my hands, which were hanging by my sides, pulled them behind my back, and I felt a knotted rope wind slowly round my wrists and draw them together. Meanwhile, the other was undoing my neckerchief. My cambric shirt, the only remnant of the man I used to be, gave him a moment's hesitation, but then he began to cut off the collar.

As this grisly precaution was being taken and the chill steel brushed against my neck, my elbows jerked and I let out a muffled howl. The executioner's hand trembled.

'I'm sorry, sir,' he said. 'Did I hurt you?'

These executioners are most gentle men.

Outside, the crowd was bellowing louder than ever.

The stout man with the pimply face offered me a handkerchief soaked in vinegar to smell.

'Thank you,' I said to him as loudly as I could, 'there's no need. I feel all right.'

Then one of them bent down and tied my feet together with a thin rope left loose enough for me to take small steps. This rope was then joined to the one binding my hands.

Then the stout man threw the jacket over my back, and knotted the sleeves together under my chin. This part of the business was complete.

The priest then came up, bearing his crucifix. 'Come, my son,' he said to me.

The assistants lifted me by the armpits. I stood up, and walked. My steps were wobbly and staggering, as though I had two knees on each leg.

Just then, the outer door was flung wide open. A frantic din, cold air, and white light came flooding towards me through the darkness. From the back of the dark gatehouse I took in at a glance the whole of the rain-soaked scene, the heads of a thousand shrieking spectators crammed one on top of the other on the stairway leading to the Palais; to my right, at street level, a row of police horses, only the front hooves and chests of which could be seen through the low entrance door; opposite, a detachment of soldiers drawn up in battle order; to the left, the back of a cart with a stepladder leaning against it at a steep angle. A chilling sight, and fittingly framed by a prison gate.

It was for this dreaded moment that I had summoned up my courage. I took three steps forward and appeared on the threshold of the gatehouse.

'There he is! there he is!' howled the crowd. 'He's coming! Now for it!'

And those nearest to me clapped their hands. However beloved he may be, a king would inspire less rejoicing.

It was an ordinary cart, drawn by a bony horse, and the driver was wearing a blue smock embroidered in red like the gardeners of the Bicêtre area.

The stout man in the tricorn hat got in first.

'Good day to you, Monsieur Samson!' cried children who were hanging from the railings.

An assistant followed him.

'Three cheers for Mardi!' the children cried once more.

They both sat down on the front seat.

It was my turn. I managed to climb up quite steadily.

'He's got guts!' said a woman standing beside the gendarmes.

This gruesome compliment gave me courage. The priest took his place beside me. I had been sat down on the back seat, facing away from the horse. I shuddered at this supreme act of delicacy.

How humane their behaviour is!

I tried to look around me. Gendarmes in front of me, gendarmes behind; then crowds, crowds, and more crowds, and a sea of heads on the Place.

A squad of mounted police was waiting for me at the gate by the entrance to the Palais.

The officer gave an order. The cart and its escort began to move, as if propelled forward by the chanting rabble.

We went out through the gate. As the cart turned towards the Pont-au-Change bridge, the square shook with noise from the ground up to the rafters, and bridges and banks joined in until the earth shuddered.

There, the mounted escort joined up with those on foot.

'Hats off! hats off!' a thousand mouths cried in unison. As though I were the King.

Then I too laughed horribly, saying to the priest, 'Their hats, my head.'

We went at walking pace.

The Quai aux Fleurs smelled fragrant, for it's market day. The flower-girls stopped making their bouquets to come and see me.

Opposite, a little way along from the square tower that stands on the corner of the Palais, there are alehouses whose balconies were packed, with the people looking on delighted to have such a good view. Mostly women. Landlords are going to do good business today.

Tables, chairs, scaffolding, and wagons were all being hired out. Every vantage point was mobbed by spectators. Dealers in human blood were bawling: 'Take your places.'

I was filled with anger by this mob, and tempted to call out to them, 'Come and take mine.'

Meanwhile the cart was moving on. At each step it rolled forward, I absently noted that the crowd behind dispersed and went off to gather somewhere else along my route.

As we turned onto the Pont-au-Change, I happened to glance backwards to my right. My gaze fell on the opposite bank, above the houses, and came to rest on a black tower standing on its own, bristling with sculpted figures, and topped by two stone monsters set sideways on. For some reason I asked the priest what this tower was called.

'Saint-Jacques-la-Boucherie,' the executioner replied.

How it happened I do not know, but in spite of the mist and the fine, white drizzle which danced through the air like a spider's web, nothing escaped me of what was happening round about. Each of these details was a torture in itself. Words can but poorly describe feelings.

Near the middle of the Pont-au-Change, on which such a huge crowd had gathered that we could only inch our way forward, I was gripped by sudden panic. Yet my last coquetry involved not showing weakness! So I drowned out everything, blind and deaf to all but the priest, whose words I could hardly make out against the background hubbub.

I took the crucifix and kissed it.

'Oh, my God,' I said, 'have pity on me!' And I tried to lose myself in this thought.

But each jolt of the bumping cart shook me out of it. Then suddenly I felt chilled to the marrow. The rain had soaked through my clothes, and the skin of my head felt wet through my closely cropped hair.

'Is it the cold that is making you shiver, my son?' the priest asked me.

'Yes,' I replied.

Alas! not just the cold.

As we turned off the bridge, I heard some women bemoaning the fact that I was so young.

We started along the fatal embankment. I was beginning no longer to see or to hear. There were all these voices, all these heads at the windows, in doorways, perched on shop fronts and lamp-posts. All these cruel and bloodthirsty spectators, this crowd, all of whom know me though I know none of them, this road, cobbled and walled with human faces... I was drunk, unfeeling, senseless. The weight of so many glances falling on you is quite intolerable.

I swayed from side to side on the seat, no longer even paying attention to the priest and his crucifix.

In the clamour round about me, I no longer knew shouts of pity from shouts of joy, laughter from commiseration, voices from noises; it was all a din that boomed in my head with a dull, metallic resonance.

My eyes mechanically scanned the shop signs.

Just once, I was seized by the morbid curiosity to turn my head and see what I was moving towards: my intellect's last act of bravado. But my body would not obey, and my neck remained paralysed, as if dead already.

I had only a side view, over the river on my left, of the tower of Notre-Dame which, seen from this point, hides the other. The one with the flagpole. There were lots of people up there, who would be getting a good view.

And the cart rolled on and on, and the shops slowly went by, and the written, painted, and gilded signs scrolled past, and the rabble laughed and stamped in the mud, and I let myself slip like a sleeper to his dreams.

Suddenly, the row of shops passing before my eyes gave out on the corner of a square; the crowd's baying grew deeper and more excited; the cart jerked to a halt, and I nearly lurched forward onto the floor. The priest held me up. 'Bear it bravely!' he murmured. Then they brought a stepladder up to the back of the cart; he gave me his arm and helped me down. I took one step, turned as I took another, and froze. Between two lamps on the embankment, I had seen a nightmare object.

But, no! I was not dreaming!

I stopped, as if staggering already from the blow.

'I have one last statement to make!' I cried weakly.

I was brought up here.

I asked to be allowed to write my will. They untied my hands, but the rope is ready to go back on, and the other part is waiting down below.

49

A judge, police superintendent or magistrate of some sort just came in. I begged him for my pardon, joining my hands together and crawling on my knees. He replied, with a chilling smile, that if I had no more than this to say to him…

'My pardon! my pardon!' I kept saying, 'or at least have mercy and grant me five more minutes.'

For perhaps it is on its way: why not? It is so terrible to die like this, at my age! Last-minute pardons are not unknown. And who, sir, is more worthy of pardon than I?

A curse on the executioner! He went up to the judge and told him that it had to be done at a fixed time, which was very near, that the responsibility was his, and that he was worried about the rain rusting his apparatus.

'For pity's sake! allow just one more minute for my pardon to arrive! I shall go kicking and screaming! I'll bite!'

The judge and the executioner left. I am alone – if you call between two gendarmes being alone.

Why do the bloodthirsty crowd all shriek like hyenas? But maybe I shall escape their vengeance. What if I am saved? If my pardon were… For surely I shall be pardoned!

The snivelling lackeys! Here they come, back up the stairs…

FOUR O'CLOCK

A Comedy about a Tragedy*

DRAMATIS PERSONAE

Madame de Blinval
The Chevalier
Ergaste
The Elegiac Poet
The Philosopher
The Fat Gentleman
The Thin Gentleman
Ladies
A Footman

---

* *Hugo's note to the 1832 edition:* We considered it necessary for the following, a kind of preface in dialogue form to the fourth edition of *The Last Day of a Condemned Man*, to be reprinted. The reader is reminded of the atmosphere of political, moral and literary controversy that surrounded the first editions of this book.

THE ELEGIAC POET [*reading*]:

>...The next day, footsteps crossed the forest dark,
>A dog the river bank stalked and did bark;
>And when the maiden fair, in tears
>Returned to sit, her heart beset by fears,
>In the cliff-top tower o'er the donjon deep,
>The keening waves robbed sad Isaure of sleep.
>When now would she e'er hear with joy
>The mandolin of the minstrel boy?

THE GUESTS: Bravo! Charming! Delightful!
[*They applaud.*]

MADAME DE BLINVAL: You end on a subtle note of mystery that brings tears to one's eyes.

THE ELEGIAC POET [*modestly*]: A veil is drawn over the catastrophe...

THE CHEVALIER[*nodding his head*]: Mandolin, minstrel, why to me that smacks of Romanticism!

THE ELEGIAC POET: Yes, sir, but sensible Romanticism, true Romanticism. We have to make some concessions, you know.

THE CHEVALIER: Concessions! concessions! the slippery slope leading to corruption of taste! I would give every line of Romantic poetry for this quatrain alone:

>'Good Bernard, there on Saturday be,'
>Bid Pindus and Cythera both,
>'And Art of Love will pledge its troth,
>With Art of Wooing over tea.'

Now tea on Saturday with the Art of Love and the Art of Wooing is what I call true poetry! But today it has to be *mandolins* and *minstrels*. Nobody writes *poetry of transience* these days. If I were a poet, which I'm not, I would write *poems of transience*.

THE ELEGIAC POET: And yet the elegy…

THE CHEVALIER: Poetry of transience, sir. [*Aside to Madame de Blinval*]: And surely one says *dungeon*, not *donjon*?

SOME GUEST OR OTHER [*to the elegiac poet*]: One small point, sir. You say the *cliff-top* tower. Should it not be the *Gothic*?

THE ELEGIAC POET: *Gothic* is not poetic diction.

THE GUEST: Oh, I see! different.

THE ELEGIAC POET [*continuing*]: So you see, sir, there have to be limits. I am not one who would dismember French verse and take us back to the times of Ronsard and Brébeuf[16]. I'm only a moderate Romantic. It's the same with emotions: I like them to be gentle, dreaming, melancholy, but never blood-curdling, never terrifying. One should draw a veil over catastrophe. I know that there are some madmen of deranged imagination, who… But tell me, ladies, have you read the latest novel?

THE LADIES: Which novel is that?

THE ELEGIAC POET: *The Last Day…*

THE FAT GENTLEMAN: Enough, sir, I know the one you mean. The title alone grates on my nerves.

MADAME DE BLINVAL: And on mine. It's a dreadful book. I have it here.

THE LADIES: Oh, *do* let us see.

[*The book is passed from hand to hand.*]

SOMEBODY [*reading aloud*]: *The Last Day of a…*

THE FAT GENTLEMAN: Madam, I beg of you!

MADAME DE BLINVAL: Quite so; it is a shocking book, a book that gives you bad dreams and makes you feel quite ill.

A LADY [*aside*]: I *must* read it.

THE FAT GENTLEMAN: It can't be denied that morals are growing daily more debased. I mean, really, what a dreadful idea! To depict the physical sufferings and moral torments that must be felt by a condemned man on the day of his execution, omitting nothing, in minute detail and exact chronological sequence! Is that not appalling? Can you believe, ladies, that a writer undertook this, and that he found a reading public?

THE CHEVALIER: Dashed impertinence, indeed.

MADAME DE BLINVAL: And what sort of a fellow is the author?

THE FAT GENTLEMAN: There was no name on the cover of the first edition.

THE ELEGIAC POET: The same man has already written two other novels... whose titles escape me. The first begins at the Morgue and ends on the Place de Grève. In each chapter there is an ogre eating a child.

THE FAT GENTLEMAN: You have read it, sir?

THE ELEGIAC POET: I have, sir; it is set in Iceland.

THE FAT GENTLEMAN: In Iceland, how frightful!

THE ELEGIAC POET: Besides which he writes odes, ballads and the like, in which there are monsters with *blue bodies*.

THE CHEVALIER [*laughing*]: Oddsboddikins! what a capital theme for poetry!

THE ELEGIAC POET: He has also published a play[17] – if you can call it a play – in which this poetic gem is to be found:

'Tomorrow, the twenty-fifth of June, sixteen fifty-seven'

SOMEBODY: That's a line and a half for you!

THE ELEGIAC POET: It can be written in figures, you see, ladies:

Tomorrow 25 June 1657.

[*He laughs. They all laugh.*]

THE CHEVALIER: Present-day poetry is certainly an acquired taste.

THE FAT GENTLEMAN: Well I never! that man cannot write verse! What did you say his name was?

THE ELEGIAC POET: His name is as hard to remember as it is to pronounce. But Goth, Ostrogoth and Visigoth are in there somewhere.

[*He laughs.*]

MADAME DE BLINVAL: What a beastly man.

THE FAT GENTLEMAN: A dreadful man.

A YOUNG LADY: One of his acquaintances told me...

THE FAT GENTLEMAN: You are acquainted with one of his acquaintances?

THE YOUNG LADY: I am, sir, and they tell me he is a gentle and modest man, who lives quietly and spends his days playing with his young children.

THE ELEGIAC POET: Yet every night he dreams up works of fear. How curious, that line came to me quite naturally. Why, it even scans: *And every night he dreams up works of fear.* 'Now I need a rhyme to go with it. I have it: *drear!*'

MADAME DE BLINVAL: *Quidquid tentabat dicere, versus erat.**

THE FAT GENTLEMAN: But you were saying that the author in question has young children. How could he, madam, if he composed that work? A horror story!…

SOMEBODY: And what was the purpose of his novel?

THE ELEGIAC POET: Search me.

THE PHILOSOPHER: I believe it was in the context of the campaign to abolish the death penalty.

THE FAT GENTLEMAN: Infamous, I say!

THE CHEVALIER: So it's pistols at dawn with the executioner?

THE ELEGIAC POET: He hates the guillotine like poison.

THE THIN GENTLEMAN: I can guess what the style is like: floods of rhetoric.

THE FAT GENTLEMAN: Well, no, as a matter of fact. Barely two pages of the text are on the death penalty. The rest is about feelings.

THE PHILOSOPHER: Then that was the mistake. The subject required cogent debate. A play or a novel prove nothing. Anyway, I have read the book, and it's a bad one.

THE ELEGIAC POET: Quite execrable! Can it really be called art, this breaking of bounds and of windows? Perhaps if I knew something about this criminal… but no! What has he done? we do not know. He might be a most unsavoury character. It's wrong to interest me in somebody I don't know.

THE FAT GENTLEMAN: It's wrong to make the reader feel physical pain. When I watch tragedies, people die, yet I feel nothing. But this novel makes your hair stand on end, it gives you goose-pimples, and then you have bad dreams. Why, I spent two days in bed after reading it.

* Whatever he tried to say, was verse.

THE PHILOSOPHER: Added to which, it is a cold and circumspect book.

THE POET: That book!... oh, that book!

THE PHILOSOPHER: I agree. Indeed, as you were saying just now, sir, that is not true literary creation. I take no interest in an abstraction, in a pure entity. I do not see in it a personality comparable with my own. Moreover, the style is neither simple nor clear, but archaic. That is what you were saying, is it not?

THE POET: Of course, of course. No veiled character allusions.

THE PHILOSOPHER: The condemned man is not interesting.

THE POET: How could he be? he has committed a crime for which he feels no remorse. I would have done the opposite. I would have told the story of my prisoner. Born of respectable parents. A good education. Love. Jealousy. A crime in appearance only. Then remorse, complete remorse, and nothing but remorse. But human laws are unforgiving. He is bound to die; and not until then would I have raised the issue of the death penalty. A place for everything, and everything in its place.

MADAME DE BLINVAL: Yes, yes!

THE PHILOSOPHER: With respect, sir, the book thus written would prove nothing. The general cannot be derived from the particular.

THE POET: Well, let us take it one stage further. Why not have taken, say Malesherbes, noble Malesherbes, as its central protagonist? And told of his last day and his punishment? What a fine and inspiring tableau that would have been! I would have cried, I would have trembled, I would have wanted to mount the scaffold with him.

THE PHILOSOPHER: Not I.

THE CHEVALIER: Nor I. For let's face it, your Monsieur de Malesherbes was something of a revolutionary.

THE PHILOSOPHER: And the execution of Malesherbes proves nothing against the death penalty in general.

THE FAT GENTLEMAN: The death penalty! why bother with it? how can one feel concerned by the death penalty? The author must be an ill-bred fellow if he thinks his book will give us bad dreams about it!

MADAME DE BLINVAL: Yes, and a churlish one too!

THE FAT GENTLEMAN: He takes us on a guided tour of the prisons, the convict hulks, and Bicêtre. It's quite repugnant. We know what cesspools they are, but what does it matter to society?

MADAME DE BLINVAL: The makers of laws knew what they were doing.

THE PHILOSOPHER: Even so, by presenting the subject truthfully…

THE THIN GENTLEMAN: But truth is precisely what is lacking! What can a poet be expected to know of such matters? You would need to be king's attorney at the very least. For instance, I read a newspaper excerpt from this book, and in it the condemned man says nothing when his death sentence is read out to him; well, I saw a man being sentenced, and you should have heard the cry he let out.

THE PHILOSOPHER: But…

THE THIN GENTLEMAN: Gentlemen, the guillotine and the Place de Grève are in poor taste. Why so? because this pernicious book would appear to deprive the reader of pure, simple and spontaneous emotions. When will the defenders of wholesome literature stand up and be counted? Well, it has my wholehearted support, and I hope that this will not go unnoticed by the Académie Française… But here's Monsieur Ergaste, who is already a member. Tell us what you think of *The Last Day of a Condemned Man*.

ERGASTE: Sir, I have neither read it, nor shall I. Yesterday, at dinner with Madame de Sénange, the Marquise de Morival spoke of it to the Duc de Melcour. They say that some lawyers are unfavourably depicted, particularly President d'Alimont. The Abbé de Floricour, too, was outraged. There is said to be a chapter against religion and a chapter against the monarchy. Now, if I were Attorney-General…

THE CHEVALIER: You Attorney-General? Let's have the people's

Charter and press freedom while we're at it! Even so, you'll allow that it's quite unspeakable that a poet should wish to abolish the death penalty. It's as though under the *ancien régime* someone had stuck his neck out and published a novel condemning torture! But since the Bastille was taken, nothing is sacred. Books do terrible harm.

THE FAT GENTLEMAN: Terrible, terrible harm. We were living in peace, and in blissful ignorance. From time to time there was a head cut off somewhere in France, but no more than two a week. And it all took place quietly and without fuss. Nothing was said, nobody bothered... Until now, when a book comes along that gives you a splitting headache!

THE THIN GENTLEMAN: How can a juryman condemn to death after reading it?

ERGASTE: It pricks consciences.

MADAME DE BLINVAL: Oh, books! books! Who would have thought it of a novel?

THE POET: It cannot be denied that books contain a poison that corrodes the social fabric.

THE THIN GENTLEMAN: Not to mention our language, that the Romantics are taking by storm.

THE POET: We must differentiate, sir, between Romantics and Romantics.

THE THIN GENTLEMAN: It's damned poor taste, that's what it is.

ERGASTE: You took the words right out of my mouth: poor taste.

THE THIN GENTLEMAN: There is no answer to that.

THE PHILOSOPHER [*leaning on a lady's armchair*]: They write things that you would not even hear said in the Rue Mouffetard.

ERGASTE: Oh, the vile book!

MADAME DE BLINVAL: Please don't throw it on the fire: it's a library book.

THE CHEVALIER: Let's speak of the good old days. Everything has gone downhill since, both taste and standards. Do you remember what it was like in our day, Madame de Blinval?

MADAME DE BLINVAL: No, sir, I do not.

THE CHEVALIER: We were the gentlest, happiest and wittiest nation. The prettiest poetry, and an unending festive whirl; it was all quite delightful. Did you ever read anything more elegant than Monsieur de La Harpe's madrigal on the ball given by Madame la Maréchale de Mailly in 17..., you know, the year Damiens was executed?[18]

THE FAT GENTLEMAN [*sighing*]: What a happy time it was! Now both manners and books are appalling. As Boileau's fine line so pertinently puts it: *By moral decadence were the Arts deprav'd.*[19]

THE PHILOSOPHER [*aside to the poet*]: Do they serve food here?

THE ELEGIAC POET: Yes, it won't be long now.

THE THIN GENTLEMAN: So now they wish to abolish the death penalty by writing cruel, tasteless and immoral novels like *The Last Day of a Condemned Man*. Whatever next?

THE FAT GENTLEMAN: Come, sir, no more talk of this dreadful book; and since you're here, tell me what's to become of that man whose appeal we rejected three weeks ago.

THE THIN GENTLEMAN: Oh, let's not talk about it here! This is a social gathering, after all. I'll attend to it when I get back to my desk. Still, any more delay and I shall have to chase up my deputy...

FOOTMAN [*entering*]: Dinner is served, Madam.

1. Ulbach was beheaded on 10 September 1827, although Hugo does not appear to have begun *The Last Day* until more than a year later.

2. Cesare Bonesana (1738–94) was the Marquis of Beccaria, an Italian criminologist, economist and jurist, whose *Essay on Crimes and Punishments* (1766) argues against capital punishment and the inhuman treatment of criminals.

3. The men were Polignac, Peyronnet, Chantelaure, and Guernon-Ranville, held responsible with Charles X for the ordinances of 25 July 1830 that provoked the July Revolution over the next three days.

4. In the sack of Troy, one of the first houses to burn belonged to Ucalegon (Virgil, *Aeneid*, II. 311–12).

5. This refers to the clumsy decapitation of Henri de Talleyrand, favourite of Louis XIII, in 1626.

6. Farinacius was an uncompromising sixteenth-century Roman jurist.

7. Themis is the Greek goddess of justice; Father de l'Ancre wrote books on witchcraft in the seventeenth century; Loisel was a sixteenth-century French jurist; Oppède was president of the parliament of Aix in the sixteenth century; Machault (d. 1750) was a state counsellor and lieutenant of the royal police, of harsh repute.

8. In Greek myth, Aphrodite brought to life the statue, Galatea, in answer to the prayers of its sculptor, Pygmalion.

9. Papavoine was executed in 1825; Dautun was condemned to death in 1815; Poulain was executed in 1817, and Castaing in 1823; Hugo witnessed the execution of Jean Martin in 1825, although the '1821' reference could well be to the 1820 execution of Pierre-Louis Martin instead.

10. Charles X dissolved the Garde Nationale in 1827; it had been in existence from the thirteenth century, and was later revived in 1830.

11. The 'freed convict' carried a *cartouche jaune* or yellow passport; the prisoner's 'three letters' were 'T', then 'T P' for his second offence; '*greencaps*' refers to the green caps worn by prisoners sentenced for between ten and twenty years; convicts were routinely 'dressed in red'.

12. The guillotine, named after its sponsor, if not inventor, Doctor Guillotin.

13. Hugo met Pepita, daughter of the Marquise de Monte-Hermoso, in Madrid in 1811; she was aged between fourteen and sixteen, and he was nine.

14. Italian naturalist and physiologist, Lazzaro Spallanzani (1729–99) published three volumes of travel writing.

15. The seven letters of his name refer to that of Charles X, who reigned from 1824 to 1830.

16. Ronsard and Brébeuf were French poets of the sixteenth (1524–85) and seventeenth (1618–61) centuries respectively.

17. The Icelandic novel is Hugo's *Han d'Islande* (1823), which opens in a morgue and ends with a hanging scene; *monsters with blue bodies* refers to the blue-flamed apparition of Satan in the eighth ballad of Hugo's 1828 *Odes et ballades*; the published play is his *Cromwell* of 1827.

18. La Harpe (1739–1803) was a poet, prescriptive grammarian, and critic; Damiens was quartered for the attempted murder of Louis XV, with a small penknife, in 1757.

19. A misquoted line not written by Boileau (1636–1711), but by Nicholas-Joseph-Laurent Gilbert (1751–80).

AFTERWORD

Victor Hugo's *The Last Day of a Condemned Man* addresses a question that lies at the core of the death penalty debate: does the state have the moral right to take the life of its citizens? By focusing, through first-person narrative, on the immediate emotional experience of the days leading to execution, Hugo presents the death penalty as not so much a form of justice as state-sponsored torture – a ritual where the prisoner is forced to oscillate between the desperate hope of reprieve and the certainty of death, a ritual carried out in the state's name. This leaves the reader with a question: what moral high ground does a state retain when it kills in the name of justice – what is the difference between this justice and the criminal act?

Neither is this story a product of fiction or a relic of the past. Today, in its various forms, the death penalty is used in over ninety countries worldwide. In the year 2001 alone*, reported executions doubled from the previous year, constituting the second highest figure in twenty years. Over three thousand people were executed in thirty-one countries with five thousand sentenced to death in sixty-eight countries. Ninety per cent of reported executions in the year 2001 took place in China, Iran, Saudi Arabia, and the USA, and since 1990 seven countries are known to have executed juvenile offenders. The methods of execution range from hanging, shooting, stoning, beheading, gassing, and electrocution to the more 'humane' lethal injection.

Yet the arguments against the death penalty are as numerous as the methods used. In his Preface of 1832, Hugo recalls the temporary suspension of the death penalty for four 'well connected' ministers. When it is subsequently reinstated for the 'common criminal' this is a stark reminder of the arbitrary nature of this punishment. Today, as in Hugo's time, the death penalty is disproportionately imposed on the poor, on minorities, on the mentally ill and those without adequate legal council. Neither is it

* *Facts and Figures on the Death Penalty*, Index no: ACT 50/004/2002, Amnesty International, 2002.

confined to the crime of murder. It is used by governments as a means of disposing of political prisoners, as in the case of Ken Saro Wiwa – world-renowned writer, environmentalist and human rights defender whose opposition to the Nigerian military government lead to his execution in 1995. And although the condemned man in Hugo's novella is guilty of his crime, the history of the death penalty is of course littered with miscarriages of justice: such as in the State of Illinois where thirteen people waiting on death row were found to have been wrongfully convicted. This led Governor George Ryan, previously a vehement supporter of the death penalty, to suspend the practice in the year 2000. It is an irrefutable fact that an execution cannot be reversed and the fallibility of all justice systems means that the execution of the innocent is inevitable.

Nevertheless what if a person is guilty – don't the public have the right to be protected? Of course. But unfortunately, the existence of the death penalty provides society with a false impression of security. Academics have found no consistent, credible evidence to suggest that the death penalty is a deterrent more than any other punishment. Texas has a high murder rate and also the highest number of executions in the USA*, whereas since the abolition of the death penalty in 1975, Canada has seen a significant drop in the murder rate.† If protection were the main reason to keep the death penalty then why would 'life imprison-ment' not 'suffice', as Hugo argues (Preface)? The abolitionist argument does not negate the seriousness of the crime or the public's right to protection – it seeks justice not revenge.

Whether the death penalty is performed before Hugo's 'baying crowd' or in shame, behind closed doors, it is ultimately a practice that brutalises society, or as Hugo eloquently puts it 'deprave(s) and destroy(s)… all finer feelings and consequently all civic virtue' (Preface). *The Last Day of a Condemned Man* is a significant and powerful part of a great canon of literature that has argued for the

* FBI, Uniform Crime Reports, 2001

† *Death Penalty in Canada: Twenty Years of Abolition*, Amnesty International Canada, 2000

abolition of the death penalty and propelled this debate to the forefront of human rights issues. One hundred and seventy years ago Hugo called for the death penalty to be consigned to history: it is only in recent years that we have moved closer to this goal. The death penalty has now been abolished in one hundred and eleven countries worldwide – but there is still a very long way to go.

– Kate Allen, Director of Amnesty International, UK, 2002

The third son of an army major, Victor-Marie Hugo, poet, novelist, dramatist, and the central figure in the French Romantic movement, was born in Besançon in 1802. Raised as a Catholic and a Royalist, the young Hugo travelled with his father to Italy and Spain. He achieved literary success early on with his *Odes* of 1822, the year of his marriage to Adèle Foucher. Their marriage later dissolved with her affair with the novelist and critic, Charles-Augustin Sainte-Beuve, Hugo beginning a relationship with Juliette Drouet (which was to last until her death in 1883). Hugo was a master of poetry, and his diction, versification, and subject-matter (including spiritualism, occultism, and notions of a cosmic framework) were highly innovative, with his preface to *Les Orientales* (1829) advocating a complete freedom of inspiration for poetry. Another preface, to his 1827 play, *Cromwell*, served to embody the ideals of the French Romantics. Hugo's novels – most famously *Notre-Dame de Paris* (1831) and *Les Misérables* (1862) – are dominated by a sense both of fatality and social conscience.

In 1841, Hugo was elected to the Académie Française, but, after denouncing Louis-Napoleon Bonaparte's coup d'état of December 1851, he lived in exile in Jersey until 1855, and then in Guernsey until 1870. Thereafter he lived in Paris. From 1876, he took little part in public life, and, on his death in 1885, he was mourned as a national hero and buried in the Panthéon.

Geoff Woollen is Reader in French at the University of Glasgow, and editor of the university's imprint, French and German Publications. His academic interests include the work of Émile Zola and Jean Rouaud, and he has also written widely on aspects of penology and philanthropy in the early nineteenth century.

HESPERUS PRESS – 100 PAGES

Hesperus Press, as suggested by the Latin motto, is committed to bringing near what is far – far both in space and time. Works written by the greatest authors, and unjustly neglected or simply little known in the English-speaking world, are made accessible through new translations and a completely fresh editorial approach. Through these short classic works, each little more than 100 pages in length, the reader will be introduced to the greatest writers from all times and all cultures.

For more information on Hesperus Press, please visit our website: **www.hesperuspress.com**

To place an order, please contact:
Grantham Book Services
Isaac Newton Way
Alma Park Industrial Estate
Grantham
Lincolnshire NG31 9SD
Tel: +44 (0) 1476 541080
Fax: +44 (0) 1476 541061
Email: orders@gbs.tbs-ltd.co.uk

SELECTED TITLES FROM HESPERUS PRESS

Gustave Flaubert *Memoirs of a Madman*
Alexander Pope *Scriblerus*
Ugo Foscolo *The Last Letters of Jacopo Ortis*
Anton Chekhov *The Story of a Nobody*
Joseph von Eichendorff *Life of a Good-for-nothing*
Mark Twain *The Diary of Adam and Eve*
Giovanni Boccaccio *Life of Dante*
Joseph Conrad *Heart of Darkness*
Edgar Allan Poe *Eureka*
Emile Zola *For a Night of Love*
Daniel Defoe *The King of Pirates*
Giacomo Leopardi *Thoughts*
Nikolai Gogol *The Squabble*
Franz Kafka *Metamorphosis*
Herman Melville *The Enchanted Isles*
Leonardo da Vinci *Prophecies*
Charles Baudelaire *On Wine and Hashish*
William Makepeace Thackeray *Rebecca and Rowena*
Wilkie Collins *Who Killed Zebedee?*
Théophile Gautier *The Jinx*
Charles Dickens *The Haunted House*
Luigi Pirandello *Loveless Love*
Fyodor Dostoevsky *Poor People*
E.T.A. Hoffmann *Mademoiselle de Scudéri*
Henry James *In the Cage*
Francesco Petrarch *My Secret Book*
D.H. Lawrence *The Fox*
Percy Bysshe Shelley *Zastrozzi*